Praise for Mollie Hardwick and her previous mysteries:

Malice Domestic

"A charming debut . . . [A] beguiling landscape of a sleepy little village."
—*The Baltimore Sun*

Parson's Pleasure

"Hardwick is an accomplished writer."
—*Library Journal*

Uneaseful Death

"Hardwick's typically fine characters and quiet humor make this as agreeable as its predecessors."
—*The Denver Post*

Also by Mollie Hardwick
Published by Fawcett Books:

MALICE DOMESTIC
PARSON'S PLEASURE
UNEASEFUL DEATH

THE
BANDERSNATCH

Mollie Hardwick

FAWCETT CREST • NEW YORK

For Dixie Dee
and the Pennsylvania Pussies

A Fawcett Crest Book
Published by Ballantine Books
Copyright © 1989 by Mollie Hardwick

Library of Congress Catalog Card Number: 88-35943

ISBN 0-449-22029-X

This edition published by arrangement with St. Martin's Press, Inc.

Manufactured in the United States of America

First Ballantine Books Edition: March 1994

10   9   8   7   6   5   4   3   2   1

Chapter 1

Pig into Baby

Rodney carefully shut the door of the vicarage behind him, resisting a temptation to slam it. Then he locked it, pocketing the key for later transference to his ex-church-warden. At the gate he turned and surveyed the ugly Victorian building, with its gothic porch and mock-Perpendicular windows.

He had always hated it, the cheerless background to his long widowerhood, to his years as Vicar of Abbotsbourne. Unsuited in many ways to the calling he had chosen in youth, at last he was free, free to return to charming Bell House and his beloved wife Doran. After all the waiting and all the troubles it had worked out, they were in their second year of marriage, and he was happier than he had ever thought he would be.

He sang softly as he walked back through the village, the little square where a few tourists were already to be seen, backpackers from the Channel ferries, staring into shop windows, eating ices or drinking Coke from cans as they strolled. Two black-eyed hawk-nosed teenagers halted to stare at him with that suspicious gaze peculiar to the French when far from home. He smiled on them and raised one hand in a papal blessing.

They stared even harder, then began to giggle. Quite fanciable, though not very young, even as old as forty, perhaps, tall and slim and already lightly bronzed, his heavy-rimmed spectacles lending him an academic air, but dressed like one of themselves in sweatshirt and jeans. No dog-collar any more.

One of the girls said something lewdly inviting in her

1

own language. Rodney's smile became even more seraphic. Doran would be amused, pleased that he could still pull them in.

He could see her far off in the front garden of Bell House, tall slim figure, aureole of short brown curls, among the lilac blossoms she was cutting—from the lower branches, he was relieved to see. In the previous years he had treated her as though she were made of the sort of precious fragile glass she sold in her antique shop, and the habit was hard to break.

His mind went back from the sunny May morning to the grey windy day in March the previous year, the day she had told him. She had driven back from the shop as usual—it was in the seaside town of Eastgate, some fifteen miles away, south of their valley—and they were having their pre-dinner drink in the panelled parlour. She went off to the kitchen briefly, returned and sat down.

"Good, I can relax. Vi's casserole hasn't burnt, though I note that you hadn't checked it." Vi Small, their household help, was a notably good cook.

"Oh dear," Rodney said guiltily. "She did tell me she'd left it on a very low light. I'm sorry, I was trying to work out how the parish could possibly raise the cash if the church tower wants drastic repair work after all. We've had just about every fund-raising event there is, except firing somebody from a cannon. Too early for garden parties . . . I suppose we could hold a Boot Fair, though." He brightened. "That's it. We could ask people to bring anything that might sell and would go in the boot of a car, and use the Horse Field. You could find some junk at the shop or in that storeroom place, couldn't you?"

Doran's large bright hazel eyes were fixed on the window, against which bare branches were tapping. Rodney rose and drew the curtains.

"You weren't listening. You were staring into space. Don't you think it would be a good idea to hold a Boot Fair?"

"Oh, yes. Yes. I was listening actually. You'd get all the dealers stampeding in when it opened and buying up the

2

good stuff, of course, but people quite like swapping rubbish with each other."

Rodney adjusted his glasses and inspected her closely. Her pretty face, with its delicate features set on a flower-stem neck, was paler than usual, and slightly drawn, he fancied, and she lay back limply in her chair, her long fingers playing with the Victorian châtelaine at her waist.

"You'll break that thing if you're not careful," Rodney said.

Doran glanced down at the thin chains of silver, each ending in a useful household article—pencil, scissors, pincushion, notebook, even a tiny matchbox.

"So I will. That'll teach me not to fidget, because it cost enough, even though it *is* a made-up piece, different hallmarks. I don't know why I wear the thing." With a sudden movement she unhooked the belt to which the châtelaine was fastened, took it off, and laid it on the arm of her chair. "It was tight anyway. The belt, I mean."

Their eyes met. "What's the matter?" Rodney asked quietly.

Doran said, "I'm pregnant. I didn't mean it, I sort of forgot, what with all the carryings-on at Caxton Manor. But I think I shall quite like it, if you will."

Rodney replied that he thought he would quite like it, too.

While they were still exchanging views on the subject the door opened to admit an electric wheelchair. Its occupant, Rodney's fourteen-year-old daughter Helena, looked from one to the other of them. There was not far to look, since Doran was sitting on her husband's lap with her arms round his neck. Once they would have disentangled themselves; now Doran merely mopped her eyes and smiled tremulously.

"There's a funny smell in the kitchen," Helena said. "I looked in the oven and there's a dish with something dry-looking in it. If it's supper, I don't think I want any—do you mind if I get myself beans on toast?"

"Not at all," said Rodney. "But if you can wait two min-

3

utes I'll open a bottle of champagne, which will either make the beans taste better or stop you wanting beans at all."

"But we never have champagne except at Christmas."

"Then switch your internal calendar back to Christmas, because we're going to have it now." He disappeared in the direction of the cellar.

"Something's up, isn't it?" Helena said, the dark eyes that lit her pointed face large with curiosity. "Have you sold something? Or has Daddy's replacement come, so that he can stop being vicar?"

"No, I haven't sold anything except a walnut commode which I practically had to give away because it was so hideous—and so far as I know the poor man who was coming here has been so ill that the church authorities have put him into cold storage—or hot storage, or something. Don't mind me, I'm not quite myself. When Daddy comes back we'll tell you all about it."

A loud explosion and a most unclerical expression were heard from the kitchen. Rodney entered with the opened bottle.

"Did you hear that? Sorry, but it was one of those intractable beasts. I thought at one point that I'd have to bite the top off. At least there *was* a bottle, or you'd have heard worse."

"Yes," said Doran, "the Bishop's wife brought it when they came to dinner. They only honoured us with their presence because she was burning to know all the inside story about the Caxton Manor murders, but they did pay for the information with a bottle."

Rodney collected clean glasses, poured, and handed them round.

"I'm just as burning as the Bishop's wife," Helena said. "What are we drinking to?"

Rodney said, gravely, "To the new member of our family." He raised his glass to Doran, and drank.

"What? What?" Helena spluttered, choking on her first sip. "You mean someone else is coming to live here? Who?"

4

"Don't worry," Doran said, "not a draconic great-aunt with a hearing aid and a terrible temper. Just a baby."

"Yours?" Helena breathed.

"Ours."

"When?"

"Sometime this winter. November, I think. I'd like to get it over before Christmas."

"I doubt if you'll have much choice," Rodney said. "Well, Helena—are you pleased?" They waited anxiously for the reply.

"Yes," said the crippled girl at last. "Yes, I am. I think it will be nice for you both. And exciting. Thrilling."

"Where are you going?" Doran called after the retreating chair. "Aren't you going to finish your champagne?"

"No, I don't like it very much. I want to ring Annabella, now, so she'll be the first to know."

"Just a minute," said Rodney. "Doran, do you want Annabella to know yet, or anybody else?"

"Well. Not quite yet, perhaps, if only from superstition. But if you could just ask Annabella not to pass it on, Helena, I'd be very grateful."

"Oh, she won't." Helena's tone was reverent. "Annabella's *most* reliable."

When the door had shut Rodney said, "Now I suppose people will be meeting me in the street and telling me the news."

"No, they won't, silly. It's quite true, Annabella *is* a very reliable, serious sort of girl, I'm sure she won't gossip. And but for her it could all have been very different."

Rodney nodded slowly. Until the older schoolgirl had come into his daughter's life and inspired hero worship, Helena's spite and jealousy had made Doran's coexistence with her hard to bear—and even threatened their marriage. The thought of an infant rival had been out of the question, then. Now, miraculously, it was indeed different. A flood of quotations from the vast store in Rodney's mind swept over him—about relief, joy, ecstasy, praise, love.

He decided to reserve a select number of them for the

5

benefit of his congregation on Sunday morning. Meanwhile he refilled Doran's glass and his own.

"A shade dry, do you think? A taste that is hollow, but crisp?"

"Like a coat that is rather too tight in the waist," Doran said. "Extraordinary how Lewis Carroll always found exactly the right words, however improbable."

"But he did know about tastes. As curator of the Senior Common Room at Christ Church he reported adversely on tough beefsteak, underboiled onions, and flavourless cauliflower."

Doran regarded him with fond admiration.

"What a lot you do know. We should have a hyper-intelligent child."

"I don't really care about that. Just so long as it's healthy."

This conversation may have influenced Doran in buying an object she found at a country sale. It was a glass display case, some two feet wide by one foot deep, containing plaster models of characters from *Alice's Adventures in Wonderland* and *Through the Looking-Glass*. She paid a price which she considered over the top for it and had it carried out to her car.

"I thought it might be nice for the nursery," she explained to Rodney. "Children are brought up so visually now, and it might just have more impact than the books. When I was a child I never thought the *Alice* books were funny, personally."

"Oh, nor did I. I took them quite, quite seriously. I used to get claustrophobic about Alice being shut up in the Rabbit's house, and having to put her arm out of the window and one foot up the chimney."

"My unfavourite bit was the guinea pigs being suppressed during the Trial at the end. They put them in a canvas bag tied up at the top with string and then sat on it."

"Yes, I know, awful. Never mind, I'm sure they got out somehow. And we needn't read that bit to . . . him, her. It's rather a nice thing, isn't it? Really very good likenesses.

6

Alice's dress is a beautiful blue, or will be when it's had a good wash, which they all need. The Red Queen's wearing dancing slippers with straps—quite right. The Cheshire Cat's a bit substantial, but then it would have to be, in plaster."

"It's showing its teeth, which cats never do."

"As in the pictures, only it looks more sinister as a model. As for the Ugly Duchess . . ."

They both contemplated the hideous face under the ermine-trimmed forked headdress. "She's based on a portrait of a real person, isn't she?" Doran said.

"Yes. Pity. Quinton Massys, fifteenth century. One wonders why she bothered to have herself painted, unless it was a revenge on society."

"The baby in the *Alice* drawing surely couldn't really be the Duchess's, even though she's nursing it."

"Indeed it could—she's probably in her thirties though she looks sixty-five. There's hope for you yet."

"Thank you. Encouraging, at twenty-seven. Anyway, she'd be prosecuted nowadays for beating him when he sneezed at all the pepper in the soup."

"I doubt it," said Rodney dryly. He had plenty of experience of child-abuse cases. "There's the baby again, with Alice rescuing it."

Doran peered at the small figure. "But now it's turned into a pig. I always wondered why it did that."

"One of Carroll's interpreters thought it was because the Duchess represented the Bishop of Oxford, the Cook the Dean of Westminster, and the Baby the Faithful of the church. All based on ecclesiastical politics."

"What nonsense!" said Doran.

"That's what it is, sublime, inspired nonsense written by a deeply serious Victorian mathematics don, who was also a minor poet. There are all sorts of theories about him."

"Including the Freudian one about his being in love with ten-year-old Alice Liddell, the Dean's daughter."

"In a sense he was, I think. You can't judge Victorian bachelors by the standards of today. Love needn't have much to do with sex, if anything."

7

"But he did say he was fond of all children, so long as they weren't boys."

"If I'd been at Rugby in the 1840s I daresay I'd say the same. No, Alice was a dream-child who opened the gates of Wonderland. There, now I'm sounding like the worst sort of Carollater—must be the corruptive effect of fatherhood."

Doran lifted the lid of the display case and picked out the figure of Alice with the bonneted pig. "Do you really think ours will be like this—our baby—even if it's a boy?"

"I happen to be a boy myself, in case you hadn't noticed."

"Oh, I had. We've not discussed names."

"No, we haven't, but I've a feeling we shall be discussing them for several months to come. I can tell you here and now that I will not stand for Tristram, Denzil, Alroy, Kevin or Fabian, in case you were attracted by any of them. Or, should the chromosomes or genes or whatever prove female, I absolutely reject Ruby, Doris, Beryl, and, in spite of their connotations, Faith, Hope or Charity. And Gloria. I trust you weren't banking on any of those."

"I wasn't. I did rather fancy Rose, or Arthur ... I tell you what." She gently dusted Alice and her porcine charge. "Let's just refer to it as Piglet until we know what it actually is."

"Agreed. Piglet it shall be. It's getting to be a rather well-rounded little creature, had you noticed?"

Doran looked down ruefully at her swelling curves. "Yes, I had, alas. I'll have to resign myself to those arty smocks I got at the Craft Fair for thirty pence each, and you won't like me any more. Who ever saw a nymph in a smock?"

Rodney gathered her to him. "All the best nymphs wore them, only with the diaphanous folds belted in. I could show you a dozen Nereides and Dryads who don't look half as slim as you will in a smock. Take that marvellous painting by Richard Dadd ..."

"No, *you* take it, and don't dare to put it up in Piglet's nursery. I know you and your addiction to fantastic pictures. Archdeacon Corbett was quite shocked by that Fuseli you had in the vicarage study. I don't want our child opening its blue eyes on such things."

"There's a place," said Rodney dreamily, "for the fantastic in this all too real world. Carroll of all people understood that. Carroll, in my opinion . . ."

Doran left him to ramble gently on, contemplating the display case, while she began to assemble the parts of a modern cot she had bought as being preferable to a genuine antique cradle, which would have been expensive, fragile and much too low. The modern equivalent was suitably traditional in appearance: not that Doran cared much, so long as its occupant was healthy.

Piglet signified its imminent arrival on a blustery November afternoon. On the way to Eastgate Hospital Doran glanced at Rodney's tense profile.

"Don't agitate yourself," she told him, "It's not bad, just a pain in the back every now and then—like lumbago, I suppose. Listen—you're not to hang round the hospital in that dreary waiting area with all those plastic-topped tables and warnings against smoking, and infectious magazines. It'll take a long time, first babies always do. You go home and they'll telephone you when there's any news."

"Yes, all right," said Rodney, who had no such intention.

"And don't, please, let them talk you into staying with me and, er, watching. Quite frankly I don't want you. I'd rather get on with things by myself. Or with a little professional help. Ow." She shifted in her seat-belt. "I shan't be looking my best and I'd really rather not be on view."

"Just as you say." Rodney had been horrified at the hospital's suggestion that he should attend at the birth in the fashionable manner. Disliking even his routine hospital visits to parishioners as he did, the thought had appalled him. He was wrought-up enough as it was, feeling the tremor of his fingers on the wheel. Fortunately it was out of season, and the traffic in the valley was light. He was at once glad and sorry when they reached the big modern hospital on the edge of Eastgate.

Doran had gone very quiet, for assorted reasons. He held

her arm as they went into the hospital, very close against his side. At the lift-gate she stopped and smiled up at him.

"I'm on my own from here. It's all right, I know the way."

"I could carry your case."

"Someone will carry it for me when I get to the fourth floor. Truly. *It's all right.* You're not going over the top on the Western Front." She kept her hand from going to the small of her back, which some invisible person seemed to be attacking with a pronged instrument.

No, but you are, Rodney thought.

"Take care," he said. Of all the miserable, inadequate, pointless remarks. "See you very soon. I hope . . . I hope . . ."

"Yes, I know you do. Go on now. Quick." She held him tightly for a moment, entered the lift, and slammed its inner door. He thought of Orpheus glancing back at Eurydice as she followed him from Hades, and losing her forever. Only his Eurydice was going up, not down.

In her face, as she vanished from his sight, he saw that she was frightened and excited and intensely concerned for him. He turned and almost ran out of the building, looking like a man whose doctor has just delivered his death sentence.

Instinct took him straight to Doran's shop in the old part of the town, near the jetty and the fishing quarter. The street was not pedestrianized, making for easy strolling and window-gazing, and neighboured by other antique shops, an Indian restaurant and a Chinese one, a shop selling fishing tackle and sailing clothes, and a prettified pub.

The shop was open but unattended, so far as he could see. He went in. Not unattended: from the back room came a radio voice speaking incomprehensibly.

Howell Evans, Doran's partner, was seated at a table covered with the parts from a clock-case, a magnifying glass screwed into one eye. He was stocky, dark, moustachioed, beady of eye and Welsh of tongue. He would cheat any business competitor, but not a friend. Particularly not Doran. Women as a sex were not in his line, but Doran was

10

in a league of her own. Rodney had grown to like him very much.

"Oh," said Howell, "there you are, are you."

"Yes. Why, did you expect me?"

"Some time." With infinite care he attached a tiny wheel to something even smaller, shook his head and detached it again. Behind him a female radio voice took over from the male one.

"Er, could you turn that thing down slightly?" Rodney asked. "It's a bit . . . worrying."

Howell took the glass out of his eye, surveyed Rodney, and switched off the transistor.

"Wales," he said unnecessarily. "Found I could get it with a bit of jiggin' round. Anyway, you look as if you'd been worried already. What's up? Time, is it?"

Rodney nodded. "I've just dropped her at the hospital. She wanted me to go home and wait, but I couldn't."

"No, I can see that. Not wise to drive when you've got the shakes."

"I haven't got the shakes, as you put it. I'm just rather— nervous."

"Funny, that. Been through it once, 'aven't you? Thought you'd know all about it."

"It was a long time ago, nearly fifteen years. And some-how it was different."

Very different. Benita had been so sturdy, so confident, a country-bred girl with nursing experience. She had told him that all the women of her family had babies like shelling peas, and in her case it proved to be true. He had never se-riously worried about Benny.

"Doran's so—delicate," he said. "So slender."

"Didn't look slender to me last time she was in. As for delicate, you seen 'er throw furniture around? I tell you, that girl can shift packin' cases quicker than a coal-'eaver."

"You don't understand, Howell. What do you know about it?"

"Oh, this an' that. Enough." Howell could have added that in the mining valley town of his origins, childbirth had not been exactly a sacred subject, and he had lived on a

11

thickly populated street. His friend, being a parson, should have had plenty of second-hand experience. Funny, people were. He shrugged mentally. He collected up the clock's components with a practised hand and covered them with a cloth.

"Come on," he said. "You want a drink, you do."

"But it's only half-past four."

"I can see that, can't I." It would have been difficult for him not to see it, with seven clocks in the room all ticking away. Howell was known in the trade as a Clock Man. Briskly he locked up, set the burglar alarm and ushered Rodney out.

"Your car parked OK? Right, we walk."

Against the bitter, salt-laden wind blowing off the sea they went through the narrow cobbled streets and alleys to the terraced cottage where Howell lived—alone, at present, though a young actor was said to spend time there when not touring or queueing at the DHSS. Reefers Cottage was modest outside, plain brick with blue-painted shutters, and the Eastgate Dolphin in brass as a knocker.

Inside there was evidence of collector's taste. The two downstairs rooms had been knocked into one, and packed with antiques, mostly of the eighteenth and nineteenth centuries. The vacant spaces left by the departure of Howell's last live-in friend had been instantly filled. The effect was lavish but oddly soothing, like the company of an eccentric but affable dowager, Rodney thought.

He subsided on to the chaise longue, a nice Victorian piece, and reflected that, whatever his present anxieties, things were less stressful than on a previous visit of his, when the presence of a notable and violent villain had given rise to a general fight which Rodney had settled by a swinging blow with a paperweight.

Howell poured scotch. For himself he poured less generously than for Rodney. He had a head for drink which had admiringly been compared with teak, but it seemed desirable to stay reasonably sober.

Rodney's colour began to come back as he unwound. Howell talked lightly of the weather, of trade, of a success-

12

ful and cunning coup he had just brought off over a heavily restored bible box.

"Wouldn't find many around nowadays, would you. Bible boxes. No bibles, see. Now my grandfather, my mam's dad, that was, he used to read out of his every night . . . How's that girl of yours taking it?"

"Who?" Rodney's concentration, after two of Howell's treble scotches, was slightly dulled.

"Your Helena. She standing up to this baby stuff? Used to be a bit on the stroppy side, caused Doran a lot of aggro, didn't she."

"Ah. Yes. Well, she's been really very good about it. We've been careful to treat her with particular affection—not that we don't feel it—but special consideration, at this time when . . . She could feel threatened, you see . . . the baby a rival to herself. Particularly where I'm concerned."

"Yeah, Daddy's girl. Well, here's hoping she won't take against the little bug—here, you got nothing in that glass."

"Nor I have. Funny. Turn down an empty glass, as Omar said. Only if I did it might ruin the beautiful whatsit of this table. Pattern? No, not quite pattern."

"Patina." Howell refilled the glass rather more moderately than before, and observed with satisfaction that not only was his guest's diction becoming slurred, but his eyes were involuntarily closing. Presently they closed altogether, and he turned his head against the cushion on which it rested.

Howell reflected that it wasn't fair for anyone to look so handsome in what might rightly be called a drunken stupor. Himself, he would have looked terrible, and snored. Very gently he removed Rodney's spectacles, which were in danger of falling off, and placed a beaded velvet footstool under his feet.

Then he went to the upstairs telephone extension and made two calls. One was to Bell House, where Vi Small, Doran's domestic help, was holding the fort, and the second to the hospital.

In the November dusk outside the little street was quiet, but for the odd passing car and the sough of the wind, funnelled up the alley at the side of the cottage. The room was quiet, only the soft ticking of a plain but charming mantel clock by Viner which Howell was enjoying before turning it over in the trade at a large profit.

Rodney slept peacefully and Howell, still completely sober, read a new encyclopedia of antiques, with a notebook beside him.

At almost nine o'clock the telephone rang.

Rodney, sitting at his wife's bedside, held her hand in a tight grip. She looked cheerful and extremely well, even in the shroud-like garment which was standard hospital issue. She nobly forebore to comment on the atmosphere which Rodney had brought in with him, as of a major distillery. The three other occupants of the small ward had noticed it and were exchanging significant glances. He was not wearing a dog-collar.

"And you're sure it wasn't too bad?" he asked.

"Not at all—excellent in parts." Though not in others, she added silently. "I was very lucky, they said, it was unusually quick, for a first one."

"Yes, it seemed quick. Howell and I talked a bit—he was amazingly kind—and then somehow it was all over and we were on our way here."

Doran made a mental note to give Howell a bonus at the next divvy-up. Her son emitted a fearful, eldritch squall. A passing nurse asked, "Shall I take him for a bit?"

"No, leave him," said his mother, "he'll calm down, he's just a bit excited, what with one thing and another, and then seeing his father. Shut up, Christopher," she added to the roaring crimson little creature in the hospital crib.

"Christopher?" Rodney clutched his brow where a sharp ache had suddenly begun.

"Yes. I know we didn't discuss it, but I suddenly thought, it's Friday today, and the rhyme says that Friday's child has far to go—"

"Actually, it's Thursday," Rodney said.

"Oh, is it? Never mind. We can't go wrong with the name of the patron saint of travellers, even if the Pope has

14

thrown St. Christopher out of the first team, or whatever. I borrowed a dictionary of names from the hospital library (you'd be surprised what a lot of interesting stuff they've got) and it says that the name was used a lot by the early Christians, even before they started making pictures of this very capable-looking man carting the Child across a river on his shoulders. So I thought you'd like it." She beamed. Christopher's howls rose to a new, frantic note.

"Abbreviations," Rodney said loudly, through the din.

"Well, not Chris, I won't have that—or anything else that might have occurred to you. But I don't mind Kit, if it comes to that, and it will." Doran's eyes were huge and sparkling, her cheeks flushed wild rose. Rodney thought of awful stories about puerperal fever, and began to shout a plea to her to restrain herself, rest, not talk any more.

But what came out was "Do you think you could ask that nurse if I could possibly have a cup of tea?"

When he had thankfully drunk it, wonderingly contemplating the now comparatively quiet Christopher, he said, "Not Piglet, then? Pity. I'd got very fond of Piglet."

"Does he *look* like a piglet?" Doran demanded indignantly. "Just because Tenniel drew Alice carrying that thing in a frilly bonnet . . ."

Privately, Rodney thought that his son did indeed greatly resemble a small pig, as gruesomely presented on Victorian dining tables. He looked closer. No, there were little features, quite fine, blue eyes like chips of sapphire, a gold-dust shine of hair. There was even a faint indefinable look of Doran.

"Not at all the sort of child," he said firmly, "who might do very well as a pig. Quite decidedly a Christopher. I think you're very clever . . ."

The nurse, glancing sharply at Rodney, diverted to him the tea she was taking to one of the mothers. Very often the fathers needed it more.

Chapter 2

I told them
"This is what I wish"

A branch of hawthorn, brushing against Rodney's face, brought him back to the present. It was May, Doran was gathering lilac in the garden, the cricket season had begun, Christopher was sleeping through the nights, Helena would be sitting O levels in the summer with every hope of doing well in them.

And he was free at last.

"Ah," Doran greeted him, "I see you're off the hook."

"Yes, I am, and the door of the vicarage is on it, so to speak. Dutton's in Barminster, being given archdiaconal coffee, if he's lucky. I suppose I ought to have hung around and welcomed him, but I couldn't stand another minute of the place. We're having him to dinner tonight, anyway."

"Er, not tonight. After all. I've got to go to an auction. Bill, my runner, you know, phoned—he's seen a Prattware dessert service I just have to bid for. It's not complete but it's absolutely irresistible—every piece colour-printed with a picture by people like Winterhalter and Frith. Delectable!"

"It sounds enticing beyond words," Rodney said dutifully. "Where is this auction, then?"

"London. Clapham, actually. I'm going up early evening and staying with Tiggy." After the exciting events at Caxton Manor in the previous winter Doran had kept up a friendship with Tiggy Denshaw, one of the Manor's waitresses, a young creature of many accomplishments who was now practising them in a jet-set Chelsea household.

"Oh, then you'll get fed properly."

"I shall get fed superbly when Tiggy gets home. Oh dear. My figure!" Doran looked down at a waist at least as slim

16

and elegant, if not more so, as before Christopher's birth. "But it's only once in a while. You don't mind, do you, pet? It just means giving Christopher his bottle and changing him and that until Carole turns up in the morning."

Oddly enough, Rodney did not mind, though he had been looking forward to some batting practice with his friend Bob Woods and other members of the First Eleven. He appreciated the company of his active, forward small son, and was nobly resigned to nursery duties.

"You go and enjoy yourself," he said, kissing his wife and picking a greenfly out of her short brown curls. "I'll explain to Dutton. If he likes he can come round and feed with me on simple fare, or he may prefer solitude and the contents of the fridge you kindly stocked for him. His wife arrives next week, anyway, so the bachelor solitude might not come amiss."

"You could always go round to the vicarage. Helena would look after Christopher."

"She would, she would," said Rodney fervently. "And when I got back she'd tell me he was looking pale, or he'd developed a rash, or something, and we should be back to the *Infants' Encyclopedia* she broods on so much."

Helena had developed an attachment for her half-brother as obsessive as her previous one for her father. Even the matchless Annabella had lost some of her charm for Helena, now that Christopher was there to be petted, nursed and talked to. It was, as Doran said, convenient and gratifying, especially when one remembered how hellish the girl had once been, but it mustn't be allowed to interfere with homework. Enough was enough, even of sisterly devotion.

She said that night to Tiggy, over their light but transcendent supper, "I wish we didn't have to have Carole to look after Christopher. She's all right . . ."

"Said in that tone it generally means all wrong."

"No, no, she's clean and extremely tidy and efficient, and when she was just helping out Vi, our regular, she was perfectly adequate. And she's got children of her own. It's just that . . . Oh, I don't know. She's a very cold sort of girl."

Tiggy, tiny, casually elegant, threw back her long russet-tinted hair and thoughtfully sipped the light German wine which was all she allowed herself to drink.

"I know what you mean. That's the trouble with au pairing—if one doesn't really like children one isn't satisfactory. Fortunately I do."

"How I wish you'd au pair for us, Tig. It would be utterly perfect. But alas. We can't afford you, not remotely. Of course, if Rodney lands some sort of super job, we might be able to. It would be perfect—you love the country, you cook like an angel (not that I can imagine what they can possibly cook), Rodney likes you—"

"Mm. I like him, too, he isn't one of the bottom-pinching battalions. You'd be surprised how many there are—even where I work, which is pretty decent, I have to flatten myself against the wall every time Sir comes anywhere near me. But I *am* expensive, Doran, my dear—I've got to be, the way things are nowadays."

"I know. Oh, well. Rodney might just be lucky."

When the following day's post arrived at Bell House Rodney learned that he had not been lucky, as yet. He had written, as soon as his replacement at the vicarage was certain, a number of letters to friends and acquaintances in the world of publishing. Several of them, mysteriously, had not replied. Perhaps they were abroad, or frantically busy. Tired of waiting, he had made telephone calls. A secretarial voice had told him that her employer was in a meeting but would, of course, ring back when he emerged. He never did. It became an object of wonder to Rodney that so many publishers could be in so many meetings, or away so often for the day in Manchester or Glasgow, or working at home and unavailable.

Replies to his letters, such as came, were not encouraging. The writer was delighted to hear that Rodney had at last been freed from the shackles. But unfortunately he himself was just leaving the firm, which had in any case been taken over. Another firm, to the writer's certain knowledge, had no vacancies, was indeed cutting down on staff. And there were hints, some very frank ones, that Rodney was not exactly in the age group from which they were recruiting. If they ever did recruit again, which, in today's climate, etc.

"Old at forty-one!" Rodney told Christopher, who was attempting to crawl on the kitchen floor, an activity strictly forbidden by Doran. "Superannuated while I still have my own hair and teeth (which is more than you can say, chum). Superannuated, fossilized, decayed, unwanted. How something is the something orphan's lot, the world forgetting, by the world forgot. Honestly, it's too bad."

He crumpled the letter which had arrived that morning from another dear old friend now eminent in a newspaper empire, who would have liked nothing better than to help, but . . .

Christopher thoughtfully extracted a very nasty-looking piece of rag from the cat's basket and put it in his mouth. Rodney removed it and threw it into the fire, where, after a moment, he threw the crumpled letter. Christopher began to howl.

"Stop that, or I'll pepper you," Rodney told him with unaccustomed acerbity. "I speak severely to my boy, I beat him when he sneezes, for he can thoroughly enjoy the pepper when he pleases. Yow, yow, yow." His voice joined Christopher's in a concord of howls.

The back door opened to admit Carole Flesher. "Morning," she said, with the facial wince which with her passed for a smile. Ignoring the noise, she picked up Christopher, mopped his face briskly with a tea towel, and carried him off. Rodney decided that he would feel better when Doran came home, and decided also that he would not tell her about the letter.

Doran, returning in the late afternoon, sparkled visibly even after the reunion was over.

"You got it," Rodney guessed. "The half dinner service, or whatever it was. I can tell."

"Well, that's very bright of you, but acksherly, as Tiggy would say, I didn't. Some beast bumped up the bidding though Bill promised me there'd be nobody there who'd be interested, and a Person got it."

"What sort of person?"

"Oh, a man I'd never seen before, who's not known in the trade at all. Private, just a punter, I should think. He probably knew nothing at all about Prattware, just thought it was a few pretty sentimental pictures on decorative plates. I expect he's putting them up in his dining room at this moment, on wire hangers. Faugh!"

"Faugh, by all means," agreed Rodney. "At any rate, you saved the money by not getting it, or them. You're looking shifty. You *did* buy something. Come on now, what was it?"

Doran went into the hall and returned with something heavy and large wrapped in dirty newspapers. She laid it on the floor, knelt, and with great care began to unwrap it.

"There. What do you think?" She propped it up against a chair in full light.

It was a wooden carving, almost three feet long. It represented a cherub in flight, the face turned towards the onlooker, the arms holding up a plaque inset with a representation of the Crucifixion. The body of the cherub was realistically painted, its cheeks and lips shining with bright pink. On its wings and the ornamental scrolls surrounding it the gilding had faded or worn off in places, but the general effect was highly colourful.

"Well?" Doran was impatient for Rodney's reaction.

He temporized. "What is it?"

"Limewood, probably South German, probably seventeenth century—these things are hard to date exactly."

Rodney could think of nothing particular to say, baroque art not being particularly in his line. "Slightly gruesome, isn't it? All that blood, the wound, the drops cascading everywhere. I find it unnecessarily realistic—I wouldn't want it in my church, if I still had one."

Doran frowned. "Yes, someone's very naughtily touched it up with paint a few years ago. But gore is nothing unusual in Crucifixions like this—it was meant to make people feel sad and stricken."

"That child doesn't look sad and stricken. It's vastly overweight and beaming all over its face."

Doran stroked one glowing cheek. "Dear little creature. Don't you think it's like?"

"Like what, a real cherub? I can't say I've seen one—yet."

"Like Christopher, of course. It's almost exactly his size, though you can see that it's meant to be more than six months old, with all those curls. I saw the likeness at once."

Rodney could not, but tactfully refrained from saying so.

"It'll take up a lot of room on the wall of the shop, won't it?"

Doran looked shocked. "Oh, it isn't going in the shop. It's for us. For the nursery."

"Oh. You didn't buy it for stock, then."

"No, I just told you. Having saved the money for the Prattware I felt I could afford this, something I terribly wanted."

"How much did the pottery go for?"

"Two hundred and seventy-five. Cheap. If only that beast hadn't . . ."

"And how much was—that?"

"Well, around twelve hundred. It's very rare, you see. There's nothing wrong with it apart from a chip or two. So I felt . . . you're looking grim."

"I feel grim. Do you know how much our overdraft is?" He told her.

"Oh dear."

"Oh dear, indeed. Doran, I've lost my stipend—voluntarily, I know, but I've lost it just the same. I've written to everyone I can think of who might give me a job." He gave her in detail the story of his friends' evasions and rejections. "There was another this morning. I don't know where to turn next. I'd be prepared to work in London if I had to, but nobody seems to want me there. So perhaps you'd like to tell me how we can afford that thing, which in any case would frighten any normal child out of its cot. Twelve hundred pounds!"

"Not really twelve hundred," she said in a very small voice, "if you reckon what I'd have spent on the iron-stone."

21

"That's just a quibble. We can't afford domestic orna-
ments that you ought to be selling as goods. I shall have to
ask you to mortgage this house, which I know you don't
want to do, but we need a capital sum from somewhere.
You'd better make an appointment with Ernest Tilman."

Doran turned away. Her shoulders were drooping, and
the corners of her soft mouth. For a healthy young woman,
thought Rodney irritably, she could give a vivid impression
of a wilting flower.

"All right," she said, dully. "I mean, all right, I'll let
Howell have the cherub for stock." He saw, with horror,
that rivulets of tears were running down her cheeks, silently. She seldom cried: the only time he could remember
was when they had been reunited in circumstances of great
stress. Flow not so fast, ye fountains . . . my Sun's heavenly
eyes . . . Trust him, he thought bitterly, to play about with
Elizabethan quotes when he had just done something not
only thoughtless but also brutal to the person he adored and
would not have willingly hurt for the world.

He took her in his arms, at which she wept properly. He
kissed her wet face, mopped it with his handkerchief, murmured into her hair.

"Please, please, darling, don't cry any more. I ought to
be shot—you can take me out and finish me off at dawn
tomorrow, if you like. I didn't realize it meant so much to
you, and yes, it *is* like Christopher, I can see it now. Of
course you must keep it. I was exaggerating—we're not in
the workhouse yet. Listen—I've got a first edition of
Lambarde's *Perambulation of Kent* that my father left me.
It's in prime condition and I don't want it, never open the
thing. If I flog that, it'll buy your cherub and leave something over, I should think. Come on, now."

Doran sniffed, smiled through the last of her tears, and
protested—but faintly, Rodney noticed. He realized that the
none too attractive carving meant something deep to her
connected with her child: what, he failed to understand, but
whatever it was he could not fight it. After Christopher's
birth she had escaped the notorious baby blues which he
had met in so many young mothers—perhaps this was post-

natal depression coming on belatedly. He went to fetch his sacrifice, the Lambarde of 1570; he was, in fact, very fond of it, but it must go for Doran's sake.

She knelt in front of the carving again, studying and touching it. Her baby, captured three centuries before, in wood. For a long time she knelt there. Something strong, even powerful, came to her from the glossy limbs of the cherub, the crude ensanguined figure on the Cross. She was used enough to feeling attraction to antiques, but seldom anything like this. Not for a moment could she have been deceived into thinking it a fake.

Helena wheeled herself in.

"Oh, you've got something new."

"Yes, a church decoration. Do you—do you like it?"

Helena surveyed it from various distances. "Yes," she said at last. "It's lovely. Very like Christopher, only of course not as lovely as he is."

"How could it be?" Doran replied absently, dusting with her finger a ringlet on the plump neck. "I'm glad you can see the likeness too."

"Shall I get him and show it to him?"

"No, not at the moment, he's actually asleep. You know, I nearly didn't get this. If the old boy had got there earlier he'd have outbid me, I know he would."

"What old boy?"

"The old man who rushed in just as the auctioneer was knocking it down to me. Well, he may not have been all that old, but he had snow-white hair and a little pointed beard—"

"Kentucky Fried Chicken."

"That, or Santa Claus. He didn't come in bellowing Ho-ho-ho, however, he was obviously furious. He started saying something about having been delayed and not having had a chance, but the auctioneer soon shut him up. Very brisk, these London auction people. He kept looking at me, and I was fairly sure he was going to nobble me and try to buy it, so I nipped out pretty quick as soon as I could. He had a game foot and a stick and couldn't hurry after me. Mean of me, I suppose."

Helena said, "I don't much like all the blood. It's so real."

"Mm. Still, better than those Sacred Hearts which remind one of the worst horrors of the Inquisition. You look pale—are you tired?"

"Well, a bit. We had botany this afternoon and I had to keep moving my chair from the specimens to the microscope." Helena's schooling was only possible because of the electric wheelchair which was kept there, in addition to the one she had at home. They had managed at first with the folding kind, but it had proved inadequate, so another extremely expensive one had had to be bought. These, and the continually increasing school fees, drained the Chelmarsh purse considerably.

"Look, you go and watch TV. I must stop drooling over this and unpack."

"I've got homework."

"Scrub it. Or I'll help you with it later. Just do as I say, will you."

Once she dared not have spoken so to Helena for fear of a tantrum. Now the command was meekly obeyed. Doran had never believed that suffering refined the soul, but adolescent infatuations undoubtedly did. Especially this latest one with Christopher. She patted the carved cherub's curls, which were really quite like her own. What an extraordinary and marvellous thing that she had gone to that auction, and all for an expendable incomplete set of Prattware.

Howell was sitting in the shop, toying with a very small repair to an African tribal mask. It was well within his range, not worth sending to their restoration man, and would fetch a handsome price if he did it convincingly. He disliked tribal art, wondering what people could see in it and why they put up with looking at such ugly objects as the Benin bronze face now leering at him. The Bight of Benin, the Bight of Benin, few come out though many go in. Sounded like Doran rambling on.

He missed Doran, now so often away on domestic duties. At the moment the baby had a rash which was taking up all

24

her time. He thought women became slightly mad when they had babies. He was not particularly in favour of them, himself, though he must admit that Christopher was attractive enough and didn't smell of sick, as the ones he remembered did.

Women. He had been up to see his mother, who lived in Machynlleth, in a pleasant situation at the mouth of the River Dovey. She was a bright, lively little woman, very clearly making up for a disastrous married life in a series of frisks with local males, not always eligible ones, who were enchanted by her brilliant dark eyes and musical voice.

Sensible woman, yet she wittered on about Doran's baby like the worst of 'em. How much did he weigh now, did he smile, did he look like his dad or his mam? She cooed mindlessly over the Victorian rattle and whistle with its coral teething stick, which Howell had bought as a christening present.

She never said, emotional though she was, how much she would have liked grandchildren of her own, but Howell knew. It was odd that, since Christopher was born, he understood about this and even wished he were not as he was.

Though not as much as he once had been. The butterfly boys, with their whims and tempers and sly deceits, had begun to weary him. The current one, Prosper, was away in London most of the time and not to be relied on to tell the truth about his activities there. At times Howell thought his engaging face to be little more real than the Benin mask, and his arrestingly loud clear voice no more truthful than anything you heard on the box. Howell was beginning to feel that he couldn't be bothered with the pain and strain of jealousy any more.

"Gettin' old, you are," he told himself.

Two seaside strollers wandered in and continued their stroll in the shop, picking things up and putting them down again. He kept his gaze fixed on them, the woman's shoulder-bag, the man's hands and pockets. He had known too many smalls go that way, by sleight of hand.

The woman muttered something to the man, sniffing ostentatiously at the fumes of best bitter which wafted round

Howell. They left. Tealeaves, they had been, he could usually spot a *lleidr*.

He turned on his radio, perpetually tuned to the Welsh wavelength. A voice was intoning about the diseases of sheep. He moved on to another station, and frantic reggae. Further along the dial he found some quite agreeable music, and stayed with it.

"Excuse me," a voice broke into its gentle rhythm. "Oi. Howell."

Arthur Hidley loomed in the doorway. He was a fellow dealer in Eastgate, middle-aged, over-sized, with drooping jowls and an unpleasantly shiny skin. Not a pretty sight, as you might say, but on the other hand nothing villainous was known of him. Howell greeted him laconically.

Hidley came over to examine the repair work.

"Nice little thing, that. I'm fond of Orientalia, myself."

"Want it? Cost you, though, most of a couple of grand. And it's not Japanese, if that's what you were thinkin'— West African."

"Oh. Too bad. I'm not buying in that sort of figure, anyway, too skint at present. No, I came to ask a favour." He drew up a frail chair and lowered himself on to it, overlapping it considerably. "This carving Doran's bought—can I have a squint at it?" He looked hopefully round the picture-festooned walls.

"How do I know? I haven't got it."

"Oh. Where's it at, then?"

Howell dipped a super-fine brush in lacquer. "Abbotsbourne. She lives there, remember."

"You mean she's keeping it for someone?"

"Keepin' it for herself, far as I know. Likes it. Reminds her of her kid."

Hidley's look was crestfallen, but his glance was sharp. "I see. Think she'd part, for the right cash?"

"Ask her. Only you just said you were skint."

"Oh, it's not for me," said Hidley quickly. "The word's got about that it's, er, collectable."

"By—?"

"Oh, anyone who cares for that kind of stuff. You like it yourself?"

Howell thought. "It's not in my line, brought up Chapel you know." He mocked his own accent. "But I'd have bought it, reasonable. Doran paid over the top—bit touched, she is, just now, they get like that. It's German, Bavarian, polychrome but chipped here and there. Probably gouged out of some church after a bomb raid. Sort of thing that'd go nice in one of the old houses round here."

Hidley seemed to pick his words carefully. "Got a very vivid figure of Superstar on it, hasn't it?"

Howell held the mask at arm's length and pretended to study it. He doubted that Arthur Hidley entertained passionate religious convictions. He doubted it so much that he decided to say very little.

"You could say that. Why not nip up there and see it for yourself, and have a bit of a bunny with Doran?"

"Right. I'll do that. Ta, mate." He got up. "Nothing come in that'd suit me, I suppose?"

Howell waved spaciously. "Be my guest. Nice little Pembroke, only it wants a lot doin', pair of big Jap vases, make good umbrella stands." He laughed heartlessly. "Tray of tourist dross, you won't find any snips in there. Have a look."

Hidley had a look, but made no offers. His mind was not on Pembroke tables or Japanese vases. After a polite show of interest he removed himself, locked his shop, and drove up to Abbotsbourne.

Chapter 3

They pursued it with Forks and Hope

"No," Doran said, "of course I won't part with it."

Arthur Hidley shuffled his large feet and sat up straighter in the delicate mahogany armchair. It was dressed in a later brocade upholstery, but he knew it to be George II. He never felt comfortable in Doran's chairs, though he would have revelled in the selling of them.

"You'd get a nice price for it, I can tell you that."

"I *gave* a nice price for it. And how do you know what I'd get?"

"Oh, Dame Rumour, you know. Little birds."

"Little birds must have their ears close to the ground then, seeing that I only bought it last week and it hasn't been seen in the trade. Was this particular little bird a dealer?"

He shrugged massive shoulders. "Funny, I simply can't remember who it was. Honest. You know how it is, Doran, you meet so many guys here and there, viewing, trade calls, out on buying trips, and there's this stall I've got at Rushingden Market. Impossible to bring any special one to mind."

"Ah. Could it have been at the Mayhurst Antiques Fair last week?"

Hidley brightened. "That's it! You've got it, Doran. I still can't remember who, but that's where it was."

Doran looked thoughtful. The Sussex fair was due to be held in a fortnight's time. Arthur would have known that perfectly well if he had not been concentrating on the commission someone had obviously promised him for getting the cherub away from her.

"Well," she said, "I can't think how whoever it was got hold of the information either. Unless they were at the auction where I bought it. Yes, that's what it must have been. Oh, well—sorry, Arthur."

His face fell. "Sure you won't change your mind? You've got a kid to keep now, you know, and trade's very poor, they're not buying this time of year."

"Somebody is, it appears. Sure you can't remember any more details—who it was, how much they were offering, why they want it?"

He shook his head, downcast. Leaving, he had a final try.

"Occurs to me, you want to be careful with these churchy things." He turned back to look at the cherub, now propped against a wall. "You hear some rum stories—hauntings, bad luck, all that. Now I'd say *he* was a bit of a jinx-bringer."

Rodney, who had come in from the garden, said, "Not exactly a description usually associated with Our Lord—or his angels, such as this cherub?"

Hidley flushed. He was nervous of Rodney. "Oh, I didn't mean that, Rev. I meant . . . you know, Celtic stone heads, bits of monuments . . ."

"Odd, I never heard of any such tales connected with Christian objects, only pagan ones. And I thought Dracula and Co. were supposed to be violently discouraged by crucifixes. Don't you feel that any vampire worth its salt and garlic would be put off by that one?"

Hidley smiled feebly. "I expect you're right. Anyway. Think it over, Dore." He nodded and left.

"I won't think it over," Doran said as they watched him drive away. "And I wish he wouldn't call me Dore—he's picked it up from Bill. Or call you Rev., now you're not one. I don't understand any of this, and I don't like it."

"No. Very fishy. You're sure you don't want to change your mind?"

She gave him a sharp glance. "You'd be rather pleased if I did, wouldn't you? Are we badly in the red again?"

"No, no. And I've got an interview with Radio Dela for a broadcasting spot that sounds very hopeful. That was the

29

phone call just now. Wednesday morning, with lunch as well. Come dine with the Red Queen, the White Queen and me, and the Station Manager."

Doran opened her eyes wide. "Oh, what fun! Will there be cats in the coffee and mice in the tea?"

"Very probably, or it'll taste like that, if it's the sort of coffee and tea one normally gets at radio stations. But I was rather hoping for sand in the cider and wool with the wine, in which case I shall certainly welcome Queen Alice with ninety times nine. I think I'll take one of the little things from your Alice showcase as a mascot, if that wouldn't be too heathen for my still-ecclesiastical conscience."

"Don't let them see it, or they'll think you're eccentric. Which will you take?"

"Dunno. The Hatter? The White Rabbit? No, of course, the White Knight. He sings a song about various professions, if you recall—making mountain rills into Rowlands' Macassar Oil, haddocks' eyes into waistcoat-buttons, that sort of thing. I could recite it for them, thus demonstrating my versatility. What do you think?"

"I think you're going to be exactly like the White Knight when you're a little older," Doran said fondly. "Just don't take the Pig Baby, will you."

"Wouldn't dream of it." Interesting, Rodney thought. Symbolism of Christopher, very, very strong. "Speaking of babies, isn't it time we got our heavenly visitant fixed up somewhere, instead of lounging around on the floor?"

"Oh, yes, please. Do you feel up to hammering? I could get Ozzy in from the garden, I suppose, but he always brings chunks of plaster down with any nail he puts in the wall. He can fetch the ladder in, though."

"Shall we need the ladder?"

"Oh yes. I'll call him."

Ozzy, the Chelmarshs' gardener and odd-job man, brought in with the ladder a powerful odour of plaster, grime, the weedkiller he was not officially allowed to use, and something nameless that emanated from his clothes, which included two sweaters, both filthy. Part gipsy, part magpie, he was a snapper-up of trifles considered and unconsidered, and a believer in wearing as many garments as could be crammed on the human frame. Since Rodney's installation at Bell House his wardrobe had been much improved by cast-offs, though the difference in their heights resulted in some excessive turnings-up of sleeves and trousers.

He put down the steel ladder, with much puffing and blowing. He was a short man, thick rather than fat, hard to put an age to in spite of his scattering of grey-flecked hair. He could move like lightning when it suited him, but affected to suffer from some extreme form of rheumatic complaint in all parts of his anatomy.

He straightened himself up now, apparently with great agony.

"Oh! Ah! Grph. Phoo. Weighs a ton, that ladder do. Oughta get yerself a wooden 'un," he told Doran.

"They're nothing like so strong. It's got to go upstairs, I'm afraid, so that we can hang that carving in the nursery. On the wall by the door."

Ozzy surveyed the cherub, and surprisingly ducked forward in a gesture obviously meant to be a reverential bow, accompanied by what slightly resembled a crossing of the forehead.

"Good gracious, Ozzy," said Rodney, "I didn't know you were inclined to piety. I never saw you at church."

"Church? No, nor you wouldn't see me at church. We got our own church, us Romanies."

"Oh. Good. Closer to Catholicism, I expect?"

"Dunno about that. Tell you what, though—that's powerful, that is." He jerked his head towards the cherub. "You watch out for it."

"Powerful in what way?" Doran asked. "Good or bad?"

He muttered something inaudible, and began slowly to ascend the staircase with the ladder hoisted on his back.

"Well, well," said Rodney, "new light on Ozzy as a spiritual being—which of course he must be—not to say as a diviner."

"It's funny he should say that, about it being powerful. I feel it myself, but I really don't know what sort of power

31

it has. If any—it's probably all imagination, or auto-suggestion. The main thing is that Christopher should like it, when he gets round to taking in his surroundings properly."

Vi was crossing the hall, dustpan and brush in hand. "Christopher? Oh, he's ever so noticing—saw I had this new brooch on this morning, what Rhona gave me for my birthday. I didn't let him play with it, though, with all the spiky bits." She fingered the dazzling sunburst of imitation gems pinned to her collar, setting off her strong throat. "Did I tell you Rhona's leaving that place she had at Billington's? We had lunch at the new Indian in Brighton yesterday and she told me she's going to work in a nice boutique where she'll get more money and less of them cats."

"Why, do they have cats serving in Billington's?" asked Rodney innocently. Vi smiled on him, an indulgent smile for a clueless male.

"The assistants. She doesn't know which is worse, the ones that's been there longer than her or these new bits of flippets with no manners, can't even speak the Queen's English."

"I'm glad," Doran said. "About Rhona's job." Vi's sister had once been Doran's housekeeper, mother to a schoolgirl victim of a sadist. Rhona deserved any handouts life might care to offer.

"Still in her flat, though." Vi perched on the hall chest, ready for an agreeable chat, though she would scrupulously make up later for any lost time. "Speaking of which, the people've moved into that new house next to the church, very smart people they seem, two cars and a party in the garden going on half the night, I shouldn't think Mr. Dutton will like that much."

"Ah, yuppies," Rodney murmured.

"Is that who they are? I thought they was called Bruce."

"Possibly that house will benefit from lively inhabitants," Rodney said. "I believe its foundations are actually medieval graves, the earliest burials known round here."

"Oh, there was nothing like that when Mother lived next

door," said Vi, then, noting a certain restlessness in Doran, tactfully moved on.

"I'm not sure if that was the most remarkable non sequitur I've ever heard," Rodney said with admiration, "but . . ."

"Yes, I expect it was. Can we get on with hanging the cherub now?"

It looked good in its incongruous environment, as works of craftsmanship are apt to do. Against the Laura Ashley wallpaper (Doran had firmly banned Vi's suggestion of dear little teddies and bunnies rollicking about) and the soft lighting, its gilding seemed less gaudy, the blood-boltered figure hung in shadow. It accorded with prints Doran had found with difficulty, remembering them from her own childhood: Margaret Tarrant's *Piper of Dreams* and *All Things Bright and Beautiful*, a Dulac or two, Dürer's hare, a Kate Greenaway and a Harry Price.

Beneath it, on a white-painted chest of drawers, stood the Lewis Carroll montage. Perhaps because of the shine of its glass front and the colourful little figures behind, Christopher's round blue eyes seemed drawn to it often. In his sensible modern cot, with sides that he could see through, he lay on his front and stared solemnly about him, most often at the interesting wall where hung the pink thing which he didn't as yet recognize for a baby like himself, above the shiny things.

"Yes, you take a good look," Doran told him. "You might as well get used to proper art now, while you're young and impressionable."

Carole thought it was shocking, the way Mrs. Chelmarsh talked to that child. All those long words and no baby talk. Vi said it was only natural, Mr. Rodney and Miss Doran being both intellectual. Helena secretly used a private language to Christopher based on that of E. Nesbit's Bastable family towards their baby brother, The Lamb. Rodney overheard some of this, but kept quiet about it. It made Helena happy and, he was sure, did Christopher no harm at all. So long as it didn't lead to the deplorable mawkishness of Fairy Bruno. "I'll sing oo a little song . . . how many hare-

33

bells would oo like?" indeed. Carroll must have been pre-maturely senile when he wrote that book.

Rodney took the figurine of the Jabberwock to his radio interview. He could think of no reason for his choice, except that the poem had seemed to fill Alice's head with ideas and he hoped it would do the same for him if he had the miniature monster in his pocket.

"Don't bother to bring it back," Carole said, seeing him take it out of the showcase. "Nasty thing, with them wings and claws. I wouldn't have had it near my kids when they were that age, I can tell you that."

"Ah, interesting you should say that." Rodney, already verging on lateness for his appointment, couldn't resist a dissertation. "Carroll canvassed a jury of thirty married ladies to find out whether the Jabberwock was too terrible a monster for their infants, and they rather thought it was. But of course it's only a comic version of a prehistoric animal, say a dinosaur. Its name derives from the Anglo-Saxon, you know—*wocer* or *wocor* meaning offspring or fruit.

"Besides," he warmed to his subject, "if you think the Jabberwock alarming, Carole, what about the monsters not illustrated? What about the Jubjub bird, which he probably visualized as a pterodactyl, an enormous flying lizard? And why was the young hero warned to shun the frumious Bandersnatch? What can frumious possibly mean—something between 'fuming' and 'furious'? I personally see the Bandersnatch as having a gigantic beak, for snatching things—or people—off the ground, and carrying them away."

"I don't know, I'm sure," said Carole. "It all sounds very nasty to me."

Vi put her head round the door. "Half past ten. You're going to be late."

"All right for some," Carole muttered when Rodney had gone. "If Trev and I'd had their money when the kids were little we'd have bought some really nice things for them, not ugly brutes like that, just because they're antiques."

"They haven't got much money," said Vi shortly. "Miss Doran depends on the way the trade is and Mr. Rodney's out of a job."

"Can't say a word against them two," said Carole inaudibly to Vi's retreating back. There had never been any love lost between them.

Doran came home that day to a jubilant Rodney.

"It worked! It came off! We got on swimmingly and he offered me a slot in the Sunday programme."

"Oh, super! What sort of slot?"

It appeared that the Station Manager had been impressed by Rodney's natural blend of flippancy and erudition. He had offered a twenty-minute weekly space in which Rodney was to talk about churches in the diocese, speaking as a layman with special knowledge, and with the brief that the emphasis should be on entertainment—"of a decorous nature," added Rodney. "Nothing too blue about corbels carved by libidinous stonemasons. Quaint epitaphs most welcome, and any lively bits of history, nothing to do with Edwin and Morcar."

"I should hope not, boring creatures. How much?"

"Well, not the jackpot. But rather nice," he told her. "It'll pay for some of the extras—and I get petrol expenses."

"I'm delighted." Doran kissed him. "Clever you. I expect you dazzled him. What was the lunch like?"

"Not, you'll be surprised to hear, prawn cocktail followed by grey steak and plastic mushrooms. No, it was rather sumptuous, a special sort of avocado and that fish with grapes thing we can't afford to give people, and *not* the house wine. Nice chap—curious name, Fontenoy, might as well be called Trafalgar or Malplaquet or Passchendaele. Seemed fascinated by you, asking me all sorts of questions about you and the shop. Collecting was mentioned, but I forget what sort."

"Flattering, I'm sure. And speaking of giving things to people, why don't we have a party?" Doran said. "To celebrate. We haven't had a real one since we were married— the christening one was a bit muted, wasn't it, because

35

Christopher was sick that day. Let's have it soon, like this Saturday. I'll ring everyone up, the Eastgate lot and the new people from that awful house next to St. Crispin's and any of the cricket team you want, and of course bank managers and doctors and such, and the Bergs from next door and Helena's Annabella and her parents and—"

"Steady on. Are we having an extension built instantly, by special arrangement with an Arabian Nights genie?"

"Well, not that I know of. I thought we'd have it in the garden, if this weather lasts. Then Christopher can be out in his carrycot and get socially acclimatized."

A surprising number of those invited found themselves able to accept, with only two days' notice. Doran took time off from the shop to throw herself into a frenzy of making easy cocktail food and mounds of sandwich fillings. Rodney laid in ample stocks of a light sparkling wine which, he said, would produce exactly the effect of champagne without the expense. "Better than flat plonk—they won't even notice the label after they've had two glasses."

"Rupert Wylie will. And his palomino filly of a wife. And so will the Bergs, considering that he's an international traveller and she models. Never mind, though, I'm sure you're right."

Rodney cast glances about him like the villain of a melodrama confiding his future plots to the audience. *"I shall put a slug of gin into the glasses of the first arrivals,"* he said darkly. "It makes an astonishing difference to the way the party goes."

On the Friday night they fell into bed exhausted. The hot weather showed no signs of a break, glasses had been borrowed from the Rose, chairs from the entire neighbourhood. Annabella had found a string of fairy lights to hang in the trees. Vi had graciously consented to attend as general helper.

"Tomorrow," said Doran, yawning, "we must be very calm. Have a rest in the afternoon."

"I'm playing cricket. That's not exactly restful, whatever people may say."

"Then get bowled or stumped or caught early and sit in the pavilion. And now," she said firmly, "I intend to go to sleep."

Rodney woke early to a perfect morning. Standing at the window he admired the pearly sheen of the dew on the grass, the first roses budding among their fresh leaves, the soft haze that meant a day of heat to come. He opened the window wider and sniffed appreciatively. *The smell of Sunday morning, God gave to us for ours*—and of Saturday morning too, an exciting waft of leisure and pleasure in the offing.

He surveyed Doran, still half asleep, very pretty in a Grecian-style nightdress of hazy blue, that left one shoulder bare.

"I could go and start setting the chairs out," he said. "Or I could come back to bed for half an hour . . ."

Languidly flinging out one arm, she murmured, "I had a most extraordinary dream. I had to take Christopher to Liverpool, by train, with no money for my ticket except an old sixpence, the kind I remember from when I was a child—and a live lobster on a lead."

"No, really? Were they going to make you pay for the lobster?"

"I don't remember. But it was all very awkward . . ."

"You seem to have managed somehow. Get up—it's too good a morning to waste. I will, as I said, if you'd been listening, go and start putting out the chairs, as I shan't be in this afternoon."

Doran smiled sleepily, and reached for her dressing gown.

Within five minutes he was back.

"The alarm," he said.

Doran looked out of their bathroom. "What about it?"

"When I went to switch it off it wasn't working. No signal light. Dead. And—someone's been in the house."

"Oh God." She fastened her dressing gown and followed him downstairs.

Someone had indeed been in the house. The hall, drawing room and dining room had all been disturbed, the hall

37

chest opened and emptied, the sideboard gaping, a book-case pulled away from the wall. They hurried down the hallway to Helena's room. She was half dressed, already in her wheelchair, coming to meet them.

"Daddy, what's the matter? I heard you running about. Is Christopher ill?"

"Christopher!" Doran turned and fled up to the nursery. Rodney gave Helena a quick kiss.

"I'm sure he's all right, darling. There doesn't seem to be anything wrong upstairs, but someone's definitely been searching down here. Did you hear anything in the night?"

She frowned. "I don't know ... I think I did, once, but I do hear things in these old rooms. And I'd have thought it was just you or Doran, come down to look for something."

"Well, I'm afraid it wasn't." He glanced round Helena's bedroom and sitting room, which were both undisturbed. Yes, she said, she had slept with her door open as usual, so that she could call if she were nervous or in pain. So the intruder would have been able to look into the two communicating rooms and see that whatever he wanted wasn't there.

Doran reappeared with Christopher, bright-eyed, damp, and as full of curiosity as a young squirrel at his unusual surroundings. Helena took him into her embrace and unwisely called him her little baby Bunny. His parents tacitly agreed to ignore this. Doran had found nothing wrong in his nursery. But when they searched the bedroom floor they found a cupboard and a wardrobe opened in the spare room next to theirs, and, in the little bedroom down three steps in the older part of the house, the door was open, instead of shut.

"So they did come up here, whoever it was, and whatever they wanted," Doran said. "Thank Heaven they left Christopher alone. I don't like to think ... oh." She was at her dressing table. "My ring!"

"What? Which?"

"My engagement ring. I always take it off at night. It's gone."

"You've put it somewhere else. Let me look."

But their joint search was vain. The ring, an Arts and Crafts ruby set about with tiny pearls, had disappeared.

"I loved it so much," Doran said. "It wasn't specially valuable, was it? Why should they have taken just that? And—oh, Rodney! They must have come in here to get it. That door knob turns so quietly. They came in here, while we were asleep."

Aghast, they looked at each other. The feelings familiar to victims of burglary began to creep over them: of personal invasion, near-rape, of something slimy having crept all over one's belongings, touched one's intimate possessions and defiled them.

"Well," Rodney said at last, "we'd better have breakfast."

After an unenjoyable breakfast Doran said, "We'll have to get the police."

Helena looked sad. "It won't be Sam any more."

"No." Sam Eastry, for so long village constable of Abbotsbourne, had at last left it. His wife Lydia had to their great joy borne him a daughter. Lydia was over forty, and they had not expected her to be able to have another child to replace Jane, killed years before in a traffic accident. But here was Jennifer, perfectly normal, pretty and sharp, not at all a ghost of Jane but a person in her own right. Her parents worshipped her, her fifteen-year-old brother Ben regarded her as his special property, much as Helena regarded Christopher, though without showing it to an unmanly degree.

And so Sam had accepted promotion, and was on a probation period of two years, acting as CID aide in plain clothes and moved to Eastgate, where the family now lived in a turn-of-the-century house with a long back garden for the pram and a swing and anything Jennifer might want which could be contained in a garden. Their old Police House was now lived in by Glen Lidell, once a very junior officer noted more for his spectacular blond good looks than for anything else. Glen had married a girl whom all

39

the women thought far too plain for him, but with whom he was very satisfied. Her name was Kate and she was a community nurse, with her own car and an independent disposition.

Glen had told them on the telephone to leave everything untouched—as though Doran, with some experience of crime behind her, needed any such telling. He went from room to room, studying the mild disorder.

"Well, seems they were looking for something," he said.

Doran forebore to comment on this startlingly original observation. "Such as what?"

Glen thought. "Something that might be in a cupboard?"

"I don't keep anything of value in any of the cupboards they've opened. They could see that for themselves."

Glen knitted his fair brows. "All large cupboards. And that hall chest. Seems like it was something big."

Rodney asked, "Why didn't they pocket the silver? There's quite a bit of my father's, including some sports cups, as well as Doran's family stuff."

"And Christopher's christening presents," Doran added. "A George III tankard, Regency spoon, porringer . . . Not to mention all my Staffordshire figures and quite a bit of Bow and Derby, all perfectly portable. And—oh, lots of other objects. You know, I've never had a burglary before—some of the others at Eastgate have been turned over, and one had most of his shop cleaned out, but Howell and I've escaped. We've been incredibly lucky, really. It's so ironic that it should happen at home."

"Mind if I take a look round outside?" Glen asked.

When he came in from the garden his look was serious.

"Your alarm system's been got at—they found the wire and cut it. Professional job, like I thought."

"Oh," said Rodney. "Oh dear."

"I'll get the fingerprint boys over from Eastgate, seeing it's a pro."

"But," Doran said, "they'll make a terrible mess, white powder all over the place, and we've got a party tonight. People are sure to come in the house. What are we going to do?"

"I'll see they clear up in time for this evening, if that'll help," Glen offered.

"Yes, it would. I'll make you some coffee. Or would you rather have a drink? Oh no, you don't, do you. Right, come into the kitchen. Oh blast, Christopher's crying—go up and see to him, will you, darling?" Distractedly she hurried off.

When Glen had left, Rodney suggested that they cancel the party.

"Oh, we can't. All those people! Though I must say I don't feel much like partying at the moment. I feel invaded, spied on, dirty. Yuck."

"I knew some people," Rodney said, "with a beautiful house and a collection of silver miniatures, like the sort you've shown me. They got burgled one night and all the miniatures went. They sold the house soon after because the wife couldn't bear to live in a place that had been defiled, so to speak."

"I know how she felt. Nevertheless, we're not going to leave this house on account of some wretched—picklock."

"Certainly not. We shall have the party—let joy be unconfined, as Dr. Marie Stopes remarked, a long time ago. Sorry, sorry."

"Don't mention it. But I really do wish they hadn't taken my ring ..."

The party went as swingingly as such unpremeditated events usually go, especially when most of the guests know each other. With the first handful of guests a groundswell of noise began, working up to a steady roar of conversation and laughter. Rodney had been right about the wine. Its cheapness might have been sneered at by the discriminating few, but its potency was beyond question.

Doran had always been faintly wary of Fenella Wylie, bride of Rupert, the young local estate agent, not because Rupert was an old flame of hers (though it had burned on a very low wattage) or because Fenella was the daughter of an earl, but because she seemed yet another stately blonde, icy to the general public but melting towards Rodney. However, two glasses of extremely non-vintage fizz brought out a convivial side of her not seen before.

Rodney, who had temporarily escaped her, watched her tossing her mane and neighing with happy laughter. He wondered when Rupert was going to enter her for The Oaks. Her language was decidedly that of the stable, he noted with amusement. He had no objection, but Denise Tilman, the wife of their benevolent bank manager, seemed to find it startling and was having to work hard on her fixed smile. She had to smile, the Wylies' account being what it was.

Rupert had already got Doran trapped under the shady old cedar tree, and she was trying to elude him, not from outraged chastity but because she wanted to get back to the kitchen for more sandwiches.

"Sorry, Rupert," she said, dodging. "Some other time."

"Any time, sweetheart. You look so Botticellian in that sort of pearly thing." He kissed her neck.

"Yes, I know. Fenella can see you."

He suggested what might be done with Fenella.

"By all means. Do. But I really must get some more food."

Vi was cutting sandwiches in the kitchen. All the other doors were locked, and the window bolts fastened, despite the warmth of the evening. Doran and Rodney had agreed not to mention the break-in to any of the guests, but it was very much in their minds, a shadow over the party.

"All right, Vi? Plenty left?"

"Plenty. More salmon and cucumber?"

"Please, it's going down well." She crossed the hall to where Christopher's carrycot had been put, in the dining room. He was sleeping peacefully. Doran adjusted the coverlet round his neck. When he woke he could be carried out to meet people and learn to cope with them. For all she knew, he might grow up to be a dealer, though she hoped not.

On her way back she paused with her tray to greet the Bruces from the new house by the church, a pleasant young-middle-aged couple with two teenage daughters, who

42

said little and looked as if they would have preferred to be somewhere else. Doran managed to stop herself on the verge of asking if they had seen any medieval ghosts yet.

She squeaked as two long arms came round her waist from behind. Cosmo Berg, of course. Seldom at home, but such a trier when he was.

"Have a sandwich," she said. "Where did you get that terrific tan?"

"Egypt." His hair was so fair that it might have been silver, and possibly was, but the deep blue of his eyes distracted one from it. "I've never held you like this before," he murmured into her ear. "I rather like it, I must say."

In a polygamous society Doran would have admitted that she liked it, too. Reluctantly she disengaged herself.

"Is Richenda here? Oh yes, I see." Cosmo's gorgeous wife, a blonde older than Fenella Wylie but infinitely more stunning and poised, was accepting another drink from Rodney and managing to clasp his hand at the same time. Doran seethed briefly. Then she gave Cosmo a ravishing smile.

"Are you home for long this time?" If he was, she would tell him about the burglar. It would be reassuring to have another man within call, and he was not one to babble. The strong, silent sort. He was just telling her that he was on a fortnight's holiday and intended to spend it at home when the fairy lights in the trees went out.

"Blast!" she said. "They've fused. It's not going to look half as pretty without them. I suppose you haven't . . ."

"A small floodlight somewhere, I think. Come and look for it with me?"

But Annabella had appeared at her side, elegant dark seventeen-year-old Annabella who was Helena's one-time idol and still a great friend. "It's all right, I brought some spare lights with me, just in case. I'll get them from Mummy's car. Oh, and Helena says can she go in and sit with Christopher?"

"Yes, of course. I mean yes, she can, and how efficient you are, Annabella—thank you. Where is your mother? Oh, with Mr. and Mrs. Dutton. I'll go over and have a word."

The new vicar of Abbotsbourne, Edwin Dutton, a small man with a face so serious that he looked to be constantly in pain, was drinking the fizz, Doran was glad to see, but seemed not to be profiting from it. Nor his wife, a too quietly dressed woman who plainly was not at ease in this company. They had come from a parish on the edge of a district with inner-city problems, and felt burdened by soul-guilt at finding themselves in this hedonistic society. Besides, Fenella was standing close by them, and Mrs. Dutton was telling herself firmly that whatever words people use they are still God's children.

Annabella's mother, Ruth Firle, a comely and sensible woman, was doing her best to warm the Duttons up. They must come over to Elvesham and have a drink, she said. "But of course you'll be there anyway, for the once-a-month service. Annabella always goes. We do hope you'll keep using the old Prayer Book as Rodney used to, we really loathe the new one."

Mr. Dutton looked even more pained than usual. His wife smiled palely. Doran decided to rescue Ruth promptly. She was moving into the group when a new arrival caught her eye.

She sped over to Rodney and spoke to him urgently.

"That man. By the gate."

"What man?"

"Elderly. White-haired, anyway. With a walking stick. Looking round at everybody."

Rodney adjusted his spectacles. "Oh, him. Who is he?"

"Only the person who came in at the end of that auction where I got the cherub, and was furious that I'd had it knocked down to me. Wait here—I'm going to find out who he is and what he wants here."

Rodney sighed. Whoever the old gentleman was and whatever he wanted, he would mean trouble.

He finished his glass of fizz at one gulp.

Chapter 4

An Agèd Agèd Man

The white-haired gentleman said that he was called something totally incomprehensible. Doran led him to a quieter area near the vegetable beds, and said, "I'm sorry, I didn't catch your name. Now perhaps we can hear each other."

For a moment she saw the flash of fury cross his face that had been there at the auction. Then it vanished, to be replaced by a benevolent beam.

"Vinadas. Paul Vinadas."

"Ah. How unusual. I don't think I've met it before. But I saw you, didn't I—at the Clapham auction?"

"Yes. Indeed, yes."

The conversation seemed to be getting nowhere, and Doran could see several guests without drinks. Rodney had got into what looked like a deep discussion with Edwin Dutton and was paying no attention to the duties of a host. Somewhat desperately Doran said, "Would you like a drink? Only sparkling wine, I'm afraid."

"No, thank you. But coffee would be excellent."

Doran fumed silently. He hadn't been invited, he had no business to be present, he was, in fact, a gate-crasher, and he wanted coffee made specially. Summoning her now strained reserves of courtesy, she said, "I'm afraid that's not possible at the moment, but I'll have a word with someone who might make it for you. If you could just wait . . ."

"Perhaps there's somewhere we could talk quietly, Miss Fairweather. It's a very urgent matter, and I have come from London . . ."

"So I gather, but I didn't actually invite you, did I—and

I do have rather a lot of guests to attend to. I'll try to have a word with you later, but now if you'll excuse me—"

Again the wave of anger touched his face, then, without answering her, he moved away. Out of the corner of her eye she saw him subside on to a garden bench.

With a social smile she prised Rodney apart from Edwin Dutton, just in time to hear him saying earnestly, "But since Coverdale's Bible was a complete one, the first, in fact, surely both the Bishops' and Geneva versions . . ."

"Listen," she said, "and never mind the Bishops' Bible. That boring old creep over there wants to talk to me—about what I've no idea—and also wants coffee. He'll just have to wait for both, and I'm damn well not letting him into the house by himself. Will you keep an eye on him and see he doesn't go anywhere near the kitchen door?"

Rodney, still in spirit with the life and times of Miles Coverdale, looked dazed. "What? Oh, him. Who is he, did you say?"

"I didn't, because I don't know, but his name's something that sounds like vinegar—Vinadas, that's it. Doesn't look like a dealer, so goodness knows what he's doing here, but it's a perfect nuisance. Do circulate and give them some more drinks—on the table under the lantern."

Rodney obeyed, though with an absent expression. He had just been framing something trenchant to say about the book of Jonah.

Doran intercepted Annabella.

"Will you be an angel and ask Vi to make a cup of coffee for that man with the white hair? And tell her the instant kind will do, she's not to go to any trouble."

Annabella nodded gravely. "I'll make it myself if she's busy. Is he someone you didn't expect? And would you like me to engage him in conversation?"

"You are an angel, Annabella—I knew it. Yes, if you can, though about what I've no idea."

It was almost nine o'clock. Some guests were already drifting away—the Bruce family, the Tilmans, the cricket captain Bob Woods and his wife Barbary, Dr. Fullathorn's wife Shelagh. Only one couple of dealers from Eastgate

46

had turned up, Peg, the husband, dressed even more like the Captain of the Pinafore than usual, and Meg wearing gold-spotted hostess pyjamas of the 1930s, with an orange-dyed feather boa round her neck and a bright pink turban. They had been conspicuous among the conventional dressers of Abbotsbourne, which was why Doran had invited them. Good for everyone to see what the other half wore. Meg had stayed on orange juice so that Peg could enjoy himself and not have to drive home.

A newish dealer from Barminster, Margaret Culffe, had not stayed on orange juice. Reeling up to Doran to say goodnight, she crashed into a flowerbed. Edwin Dutton and Rodney retrieved her massive form from where it lay prone among aubretia and primula denticulata.

"Thanks," she said, holding on to the arms of both. "Silly of me. Couldn't see the edge. Glasses ought to go lighter at night, but don't. Funny thing, must be my ears. I mean eyes." She laughed merrily and addressed a spot somewhere over Doran's right shoulder. "Goodnight, then, so kind of you."

"I don't think, you know," said Rodney, "that you ought to drive home. It is getting dark, and your glasses, as you say . . ."

Doran shot him an anguished look. To have a drunk on their hands overnight, what with all the clearing up and the maddening Mr. Vinadas to deal with. In the distance she could hear Christopher shrieking. But it was true, the woman was incapable. She looked wildly round for help.

"We'll take her home with us, if you like," offered Celia Dutton. "It won't be any trouble, really—you know what a lot of rooms there are at the vicarage."

Doran hesitated. "Are you sure?"

Edwin said, "Of course. Celia and I are quite used to dealing with—"

Rodney broke into a sudden artificial cough. Celia Dutton at least took the hint, and said, "We'll be having a little supper ourselves, so Mrs. Culffe can have some with us. She'll be quite hungry by then, I expect."

Doran felt that, on the contrary, she would be violently

47

sick before then. It was imperative to get her off the premises before that happened.

"Well, if you're quite sure," she said hastily. "It's very kind of you. Can you manage? Goodnight."

With intense relief she saw the Duttons leave, Margaret wavering between them. This was how it was going to be: they would be everlastingly kind, helpful, doing the right thing, and monumentally tactless and boring.

"There's charity for you," Rodney said.

"Yes, true nobility. I do hope someone's coping with Christopher. Yes, he's stopped. The Wylies and the Bergs are going to stay and stay. Will you go and shift them? No, leave it to me. You start clearing up as noisily as you can. Annabella and Ruth have done quite enough, and Simon's sitting in the car looking impatient. Enough's enough of a party."

The Wylies and the Bergs reluctantly disentangled themselves from their drinks, and each other. No exchange of partners had been effected, evidently, though Doran suspected that all four had had something of the kind in mind. How fortunate that they could walk home.

She switched off the fairy lights. The garden was dark and quiet, but for a few very late birds twittering languidly. The twilight thrush who sang his full-throated nightingale song every evening had rendered it, and gone home. The tulip tree in the Bergs' garden was a great candelabrum of bloom in the dusk. How pleasant to have space where there had been people, peace after chatter.

But Mr. Vinadas sat on, in the shadows near the vegetable garden.

Doran pointed him out to Rodney, who was passing with the last of the trays of empty glasses and paper plates.

"Not still there? The foul fiend fly away with him."

"I wish it would, but it won't. I shall have to tackle him myself."

Vinadas impassively watched her coming towards him, not rising to his feet. She stood over him.

"Mr. Vinadas, what is it you want? Can you tell me

48

quickly, please, because I'm very tired and my husband and I want to lock up and go to bed."

His eyes gleamed up at her in the dusk; with his large head and white hair that grew out in tufts, one at the top, two at the sides, he looked not unlike the Ghost in Lewis Carroll's *Phantasmagoria: something white and wavy standing near me in the gloom.* Only he continued to sit.

"The limewood carving of a *putto*, bought by you at Stockwood's auction. I want to buy it."

"I thought so. That's why you're here, isn't it? Well, the answer is that I'm not selling it."

"You are an antique dealer, I believe, madam."

"I am. But as it happens I'm keeping this particular antique."

"So I heard from your, er, colleague. I called at your shop as it was closing this afternoon. He directed me to come here."

The rat, thought Doran. He might at least have rung and warned me. He knew I'd be at home, because he was invited to the party. Aloud she said, "I'm sorry you've had the trouble of coming all this way, because, quite definitely, I am not selling this piece. I do remember you at the auction, and I expect you found out there where I traded. If I were you I should drive back to Eastgate for the night—it's quite a distance to London, and the valley roads are very twisty."

He sat on, still looking fixedly up under his brows.

"I came here by taxi—a very expensive way of travelling," he said. "I have no transport."

Doran stared at him, dismayed.

Rodney was not to be seen in the garden, but she found him in the kitchen, cramming debris into an already full bin.

"Listen—he won't go. He hasn't a car, he came by taxi from Eastgate. What am I to do with him?"

"Send him back by taxi. Ring Valley Cars."

"It's not that, though I don't think he'd pay. He just won't go, he wants me to sell him the cherub and he's going to be bloody-minded about it, I can see that."

49

"Don't expect me to offer to drive him back, that's all. I've had a few drinks and I'm not losing my licence for anybody, especially a gate-crasher. I shall take Vi home, and that's it. Vi! Come on."

"Just seeing Helena into bed," a faint reply floated from the rooms at the end of the hall.

Doran, walking up and down with Christopher, who had turned fretful, wondered what she could possibly do. Certainly not pay for a mini-cab to take Vinadas fifteen miles, always supposing he would agree to go. A room at the Rose? That would cost quite enough, and the Bellacres wouldn't thank her for bringing them a bed-and-breakfaster late on a Saturday night. He could hardly be added to the vicarage guest-roll, that would be unfair to the Duttons.

Vi appeared. "That old gentleman out in the garden, I saw him from Helena's window. Looks like he'll be staying, unless he's waiting for someone to fetch him—anyway, I made the attic spare up for him, just in case."

Doran began, "Oh, Vi, really—if you'd just asked me first."

"It seems that we're meant to take the stranger in," Rodney said. "I only hope it's safe. He didn't look as if he might get violent, did he?"

"No, I don't think so—too infirm. Well, all right, but I don't like it."

She went out to the garden again, Christopher against her shoulder. Vinadas seemed not to notice Christopher.

"Mr. Vinadas, since you've no means of transport I've no choice but to offer you a room for the night. I must say at this point that I very much resent having to do that, since I didn't invite you here and it's absolutely useless for you to argue with me about what you want. The room is in our attics, rather a lot of stairs, I'm afraid." She glanced at his stick. "But it's all there is. And I shall expect you to leave early tomorrow."

He had the grace to thank her. Stiffly he got up and followed her into the house. She put him in the dining room, where, she noticed, he gazed eagerly round the walls. She

50

then locked the drawing room door from the outside, just in case he had thought of making a search.

By the time she had put Christopher to bed Rodney was back. They met in the kitchen.

"Well?" he asked her. She told him what she had done.

"It's the greatest possible nuisance. I hate being pestered at home, and I don't care for the old—gentleman. But at his age, and with an infirmity, what can I do?"

"He is really old, I suppose? I mean it's not a brilliant disguise, athletic young villain masquerades as snowy-locked patriarch? *You are old, Father William, the young man said, and your hair has become very white*—that sort of thing?"

Doran laughed in spite of her irritation. "At least he doesn't incessantly stand on his head—yet. I think he's middle-aged going on old. Oh well. I don't know about you, but I''m hungry."

"I'm starving. Those insubstantial cocktail bits go no-where, especially when one's talking. What have we got?"

"Eggs and bacon." The cat Tybalt got out of his basket, elongating himself in each direction twice, and gazed up at Doran with lambent eyes.

"All right, all right," she said. "Food for all. Cold fish for you, Tybalt. Thank heaven Christopher wasn't pernick-ety about going to bed tonight."

As she was laying the kitchen table she paused.

"I suppose we ought to ask—him. It seems hardly decent not to."

Rodney looked less than enthusiastic. "Certainly. We must, oh dear. I'll get him."

Vinadas paid no attention to Doran's unusual kitchen, the fine eighteenth-century dresser where Staffordshire figures stood among everyday cups, saucers and plates, the modern sink over which played Oberon and Titania and some well-developed fairies, painted on tiles for the Minton factory a hundred years before. He said no word of thanks for his supper, but ate it wolfishly, without seeming to taste it. Sometimes he smiled briefly at them, switching the smile off like a light. His plate was clear long before either of theirs.

He laid down his knife and fork and said, "The carving. Where is it?"

"Not really any business of yours," said Doran, in her gentlest voice to soften the words.

"But in this house."

Doran said nothing.

"I must have it, you see. My collection is absolutely incomplete without it."

"Oh, you're a collector?"

"Of—what I might call *religiosi.* Tokens from all religions. I have a large room full of showcases. A gilded bronze of Sekhmet, goddess of cats, with seven kittens. A marble figure of Venus holding the apple and mirror. A vase depicting the birth of the monster Typhon to Hera. Lakshmi in ivory, seated on a lotus. A Jizo Bosatsu from the thirteenth century, in wood with decoration of gold and pearl. A sarcophagus from the Upper Nile. The Great Goddess of the ...."

Rodney felt an invisible dog-collar tightening round his neck. Doran said, *"Religiosus, a, um?"*

Again the pocket-torch smile. "Very erudite."

"Are any of these *religiosi* Christian?" Rodney inquired.

"A great many images, of course, too many to describe—statues, paintings, icons, the usual objects. That makes the object you have temporarily in your possession quite unique and indispensable to me. You see?" He looked from one to the other with an air of triumph.

"But you haven't said what it is," Doran pointed out. "It looks to me like a fairly usual church decoration from somewhere in—oh, I don't know, Rumania, Bulgaria."

"Spain."

"Spain, then. I don't see that it matters. To me, it's beautiful, but some people"—she glanced at Rodney—"don't like it. You still haven't said what it is."

Vinadas looked her solemnly in the eye. "It is a piece of the True Cross."

Doran's swift turn of the head towards Rodney said, "Your bird, sir."

"Can you give us a little background?" Rodney inquired. "Date of discovery, authentication, site of . . ."

Vinadas interrupted. "It was found by Protonice, wife of the Emperor Claudius."

Rodney started to ask which of Claudius's wives she might be, but was interrupted again.

"History does not know the precise date of the Empress's finding of it, but it must have been prior to the year 42 when Claudius was certainly under the influence of Messalina, his third wife."

"Claudius didn't become Emperor until 41," said Rodney. "Nobody was all that interested in him before that date. It surprises me to know that a discovery by some young woman he happened to be married to then, and who was definitely not an Empress, caused any comment. Besides, the finding of the Cross, if that's what it is, is generally attributed to Helena, mother of the Emperor Constantine, in 326. I know, because my daughter's called after her."

"In 326, you said." Vinadas smiled smugly. "The fourth century AD is a long time after—shall we say—a date before 42 AD. It is, in fact . . ."

Doran's mind had been working, and she could tell that Rodney's had. The Crucifixion had taken place in 30 AD. So there was a gap of only twelve years, or even as much as that? She felt a sudden frisson.

Rodney asked, "Where was this object—found?"

"It was never lost. A Roman centurion was converted at the foot of the Cross. He cut a piece of it off with his sword and took it back to Rome with him, where he kept it as a holy relic. Of course, the news got back to the authorities, and Protonice went to look into the affair."

"Inquisitive girl."

"Yes. The soldier met with the usual fate—the lions, I believe—but Protonice seems to have escaped punishment."

"And she kept the piece of wood. From the execution a very few years before."

"She did. Stories began to circulate immediately."

Doran said, "You're not trying to tell us that this carving is all carved from the actual Cross? I'd hardly imagine they'd have used limewood for that. It's a soft, light wood, fine for ornamental carving but not ideal for—well, gallows. Besides, this is obviously not more than three centuries or so—"

"I said nothing of the kind," Vinadas snapped. "I said that it *incorporated* a piece of the *Crux Imissa*. I assume it to be incorporated in the plaque displayed by the *putto*."

"Not actually a *putto*, is it—" Doran began, but Vinadas was rushing on.

"If I could examine it. The light in this room is very poor"—he glanced disparagingly at a charming Art Nouveau bronze figure of a nymph holding a lamp—"but I expect I could see all I need. That auctioneer was quite wrong, quite wrong not to listen to me when I told him clearly that I had the best claim to the carving—the man can't have heard me."

"He heard you, all right," Doran said. "We all did. He had just sold it to me, because you weren't there in time, and auctions aren't about laying claim to things. And now, Mr. Vinadas, I'm going to take you up to your bedroom. I must ask you to stay in it, please, and not wander about, because our baby wakens rather easily and we have a delicate daughter who must have her sleep."

He was not pleased to be led, limping, up so many stairs, but as he went he scanned the walls avidly. Doran, polite only by an effort, would have liked to lock him in, but there was no bathroom on the attic floor. In view of his possible excursions during the night, she locked the nursery door from outside and their own bedroom from inside, keeping the nursery key under her pillow in case they heard Christopher crying on the baby-alarm.

They undressed almost in silence, too tired for much discussion.

"Short on charm, Mr. Vinadas," Rodney observed.

"Very. To say the least. Could there be anything in this story, or is he mad?"

54

"There have been millions of pieces of the Cross found," Rodney said, hurling his jacket across the room. "Medieval churches and abbeys were packed with them—also with fingers of John the Baptist, hems from Our Lady's robe, rods of Moses, phials of holy blood, the Magdalene's hair, and enough bones to stock several cemeteries. Who knows? His version might be true. One chap, according to the Cistercian community at Vale Royal, undoubtedly went through the Crusades quite unscathed because he carried a bit of the Cross round his neck. I really don't know. Let's go to bed, shall we?"

"So you won't let me see it?" Vinadas asked next morning. Doran had taken him a tray of breakfast to keep him out of the way. Rodney had gone to the eight o'clock Communion; Helena was giving Christopher his bottle.

"No, I won't. I don't intend to sell it to you or to anybody else."

He eyed her spitefully. "You're doing a very immoral thing, young woman, standing between a serious collector and the objects he understands and values more than any amateur possibly can. Let me tell you I have been collecting *religiosi* since I was a boy of ten." He reeled off what seemed like an interminable list of them, and of the travels he had undertaken in their pursuit, while Doran surreptitiously looked at her watch, noted that the Bergs' curtains were not drawn yet, wondered whether she should have ordered an extra pint of milk, frowned at a patch of damp on the wall, and remembered that the dealer John Pink was calling for her early next morning.

Vinadas had stopped talking and was getting dressed. Doran withdrew. When she looked in again he was as he had been the previous evening, wearing an unattractive suit. She was sure, seeing him in full daylight, that he was not a truly old man but a prematurely white-haired one, with a pedantic manner.

"Two thousand," he said. "I offer you two thousand pounds."

"I paid twelve hundred. I could get twice that in the right

55

market, if I were selling—but I'm not. How do you propose to get home?"

He seemed to have no idea, and to be uninterested in getting home at all.

"Right. My husband will drive you into Eastgate when he gets back from church, and you can get a train from there."

Until the very last moment Vinadas lingered in the hall, darting famished glances about him at closed doors. He was, Doran thought, like a stoat in a burrow, furiously knowing that the rabbit is holed safely at the end of it, but unable to get there.

As he left the house she said sweetly, "Oh, Mr. Vinadas. Did you burgle our house recently?"

He glared. "Burgle your house? What do you think I am, madam?"

A lunatic. A collector of specialist-market stuff. An obsessional neurotic. A gate-crasher. Oh well, never mind, he's gone.

She thought, as he looked back at her from the garden path, that his lips had formed the words, "I curse you."

Chapter 5

You may charge me with Murder . . .

Arthur Hidley was hovering.

Doran could see him out of the corner of her eye, as she had almost got her buyer to the point of non-resistance to a Derby sauceboat with a few chips and a hairline crack. Doran had in honour bound pointed out these defects, which the customer, an early tourist, seemed not to mind too much, but he was wavering on the brink.

"Well . . ." he said. "Lot of money."

"It would be more than two hundred if it were perfect—as it is, you're getting it cheap."

Hidley gave an artificial cough and shuffled slightly forward, dislodging a japanned box which fell on to a set of fire irons, causing a clatter. Doran swore mentally. The customer jumped, gave a nervous smile, and murmured something, backing away as he did so, until he was almost at the door. Doran, working out her lost percentage of profit, watched him go. Hidley advanced on her, and she turned, angrier than he had seen her before.

"That was your fault, Arthur. I've lost a good sale, and we need every penny we can make, as well you know. What do you want, anyway? If it's the shop to be minded, I can't—Howell's away buying and I daren't leave with all that new stuff in the window. You *are* a nuisance."

"Sorry, Doran, sorry. I didn't know he was a punter."

"Who did you think he was, the Lord Lieutenant?"

Hidley fiddled with a Victorian bead purse, not looking at her. She took it out of his hand and put it out of reach.

"If you pull at those beads they'll break and then it won't be worth anything. Well?"

He met her eyes. Not for the first time she thought that his were like those of a very large stuffed pike.

"Er, Doran. Won't you change your mind about that thing you're hanging on to, the carving? I've had a great offer, one you can't refuse—twice as much as it's worth."

"Oh? How much?"

"Two grand with the understanding that you're bound to up it a bit, or even a lot. How about that?"

Two thousand. Exactly what Vinadas had offered, only he had made no mention of upping it.

"And you get a cut, of course?" she said.

"Well, a bit of commission, that I'm entitled to. I've got to live, you know, Doran. I won't take much, I promise. You could even keep the cash for yourself as Howell's away, and after all the thing is yours."

"What a rat-like suggestion." Doran's voice was cold. She had just seen the escaped customer going into the shop across the street, which had recently opened and was selling nasty modern imports along with a few antiques. Her heart was hardened. "Once and for all, I'm not going to sell that carving. I've had that much offered for it already, and refused. And who's making this offer? You told me you couldn't remember the name of the person who was interested in it, and you also told me that you'd met him or her or them at a fair which in fact hadn't taken place. It all sounds very fishy to me, and I won't have anything to do with it."

Hidley turned an unbecoming shade of crimson plush, and twitched with embarrassment.

"I'm sorry, Doran. I got a bit mixed up. One of those things, you see, buyer doesn't want to be known—personal reasons, sort of. I can't really tell you, but the offer's genuine, honest it is." If a stuffed pike's eyes could plead, his pleaded.

"I'm sorry, too, but I don't do business that way." An unpleasant thought struck her. "The carving isn't hot, by any chance—it's not on the police list? Because if it is I'll report it at once."

"No, no, of course it isn't. Would I touch it if it was?

Would any of us? Look, think over what I've said. It's absolutely kosher and I can get you cash as soon as you hand the thing over. You'll go off it in time, Dore, I know you, you've just got a temporary fancy for it. Howell even said . . ."

"Well, go on. What did Howell say?"

It was impossible for him to flush a deeper colour.

"Only that, er, you're not quite, er, yourself yet."

"Meaning," said Doran grimly, "that I've had a baby and gone peculiar, as we poor female nitwits are well known to do? Thank you, both of you. You can tell your mysterious buyer that we can be very stubborn, demented as we are, and that it's all the wonderful work of Nature and completely out of your hands. Understood?" She turned her back on him and began to arrange a set of marbles in order of size.

On the way home she felt a twinge of remorse. Hidley was not really bent: one couldn't blame him for wanting a bit of commission, and some characters in the collecting world were very quirky. And then there was the electricity bill, and the telephone bill, and the rate increase in Eastgate, and Carole's wages, which regularly drained the housekeeping money. Perhaps she'd been over-hasty.

But against the line of traffic moving down the narrow road that led to the valley she pictured the cherub, its pink apple cheeks, its celestial smile, the curls so like her own, and Christopher growing and playing and sleeping under its benign influence. She would not part with it.

The telephone call came a few days later.

"Yeh," said Howell, answering. "Hold on." He beckoned Doran over.

"Who is it?"

"Some woman."

The voice was unknown to Doran, a pleasant well-modulated voice, classless, neither young nor old.

"Miss Fairweather? I'm so glad I caught you in the shop. You won't know me—my name's Page, Hanna Page, spelt H-a-n-n-a, and I'm a dealer of sorts."

"Oh yes?" Doran was cautious of unknown dealers. "How can I help you?"

"Well. I'm trying to start up in Barminster—looking at premises, all that, you know, what a business it is, and the rents, so horrific. I just wondered, while I'm here, whether we could meet. I've got a little stock in the car and I'd like you to see something that might be in your line."

"How did you hear of me?"

The woman laughed. "Oh, don't be so modest, you're more famous than you think. People talk, fairs, markets, you know . . . Well, what about it—can we meet?"

"When?"

"I thought perhaps today. I have to go back to Cheshire tomorrow."

Trade was slack. Howell would be in the shop all day—their furniture restorer was calling, so he would not be able to escape to the pub for too long. And, tied as she usually was at home, Doran rather fancied an interlude in Barminster, the cathedral city which always gave her a spiritual lift, even its modern shopping area, which was full of tempting things. Without too much pressing she agreed to meet Hanna Page in a small restaurant near the cathedral for a light lunch.

Hanna Page's appearance was reassuring. Slender, fortyish—or could it be fiftyish?—her really rather pretty face and cleverly russet-tinted hair met with Doran's approval, as did her well-cut frock of amber linen.

"I'm so pleased to see you," she said as they seated themselves at a corner table in the little dining room where real upright beams and rafters were discreetly backed up by fake ones, and the fireplace of Stuart brick was not, unlike most, cluttered up with horse brasses which had never seen the inside of a stable.

Strange dealers were not, on the whole, given to saying that they were pleased to see one, or admiring the cream suit, old but favourite, which one happened to be wearing. Doran relaxed, and accepted a glass of wine with the meal, which Hanna Page insisted was down to her because she'd dragged Doran away from the shop. They talked about Barminster, premises, rents, rates, Abbotsbourne, which

Mrs. Page (the rings which clustered on her fingers included a plain gold one) knew slightly and admired, about Rodney, and about Christopher.

"You don't know how I envy you." Hanna looked into her wine glass, unseeingly. "I shall never have a child, now. My marriage cracked up, and I'm too old anyway. You're lucky, so lucky."

"I know. He's wonderful." Doran found herself laying out snapshots on the table, pointing out the changes during Christopher's few months of life, his precocious strength and brightness, the sunniness of his smile.

She wasn't able to resist showing Hanna the cherub, in its prestigious position on the wall.

"I don't know whether you're into carved wood of this sort—some people aren't though it's fetching a bomb nowadays, even hideous-looking John the Baptists and very plain saints. But I adore this one, somehow. To me it's Christopher: a sort of spiritual emanation of him. And very beautiful in itself, don't you think—what you can see of it?"

"Mm. It does look very handsome. I'm not actually into baroque myself, I mean I really don't know anything about it—but a friend of mine is, very much so. You could get a lot of money for this, you know, if you'd let me . . . *Would* you let me drop a word?"

Hanna's eyes, in their contact lenses, were as full of hope and pleading as though she were certain of an enormous commission on such a sale.

"I'm sorry, I wouldn't consider it. I've already had a good offer. No, this I'm keeping for myself. I'm sure you understand that. As a dealer you must often have found something you couldn't bear to sell. It's so like Christopher, you see."

"The ringlets look a bit—well, for a baby of any age . . ."

"Oh, Christopher will do better than that," Doran said blithely. "He was almost bald when he was born, just a sort of almost invisible crew-cut, but now you can see he's going to have curly hair, just like . . ."

"Just like yours. Lucky Christopher. Lucky Doran." She sighed, and gazed at the snap in her hand. It had been taken with a flash in the nursery. Christopher's cot was in the centre, with Christopher rearing himself on his hands, his face lit with laughing wonder at the bright light. Hanna propped the photograph against the flower vase and contemplated it, with longing in her eyes.

Doran was flattered, basking vicariously in another woman's admiration of her son. But one mustn't gloat over someone less happy than oneself. And she had come to meet Hanna for a reason. She forced herself away from her favourite subject.

"You said you had something to show me."

Hanna, too, seemed to detach herself with difficulty from the image of Christopher. "Of course. It's in the car—I'll get it."

Like Doran, she had parked in the space provided behind the restaurant, almost under the shadow of the cathedral's west towers. In a moment she was back with a canvas flightbag, in which she searched, leaving the bag on the floor.

"Oh, these bits of newspaper! I don't want to scatter them all over the carpet. What a blessing there's almost nobody here. I'm so inept." This was true.

"Let me." Doran knelt and disinterred a porcelain figure, which she placed on the table.

"Minerva? Judging by the helmet. Early Chelsea-Derby?" With a sure professional touch she upturned it and examined the mark on the base.

"Oh dear. Gold anchors, but definitely not Chelsea-Derby. S logo, but not Samson of Paris. Alas, it's a fake of a fake, not Samson imitating Chelsea but somebody not very long ago imitating Samson."

Hanna Page appeared stunned.

"Oh. I've been properly taken in, then."

"Possibly you're new to porcelain." Doran felt as guilty as though she, personally, had manufactured the thing, for the putting-down of this innocent, even naïve, victim. "It's odd that a firm like Samson, started as late as 1845 to make

62

replacements of matching wares, should first have got so big and then become collectable in their own right—and now they're even being copied, and sold at auction. Blatant, really. It just shows what a tacky game this is, even though we love it. You *are* new to it, aren't you?"

"Yes," Hanna said. "I'm sorry, I did try to put on a front. But I am, fairly new. I had to make a life for myself and I thought this would be an attractive sort of environment. I'm afraid there's a lot I don't know. Do put that thing away."

Doran asked the waitress for coffee, re-wrapped the simpering goddess and re-packed the flight bag. She was very sorry for this lonely woman, who had neither family nor established profession. She talked, keeping it light, of other matters; Barminster again, lovely and ancient and badly bombed, its matchless cathedral, the so-called developers who had jumped into Hitler's footsteps and flung up multi-storey car parks and tower blocks of offices that nobody wanted. Of Kent, and clothes, and stray cats, and practically everything except the antiques trade.

Yet it kept cropping up. "You must make a lot of money," Hanna said wistfully.

"Good heavens, no. I just keep ticking over. If it wasn't for my partner's business brains I'd be out on my ear by now. As it is, we're in the red more often than not, but he's marvellous, and we keep going. Well, I have to—my husband hasn't got a job at the moment and we need every penny. Not that I mind. But you haven't told me anything about yourself—how awful, I've just been going on at you. Where did you begin?"

Hanna shrugged. It was a plain tale, or she kept it so. A beginning in Berkshire, an advertising job in London, marriage and removal to Manchester, then rural Cheshire, then the collapse of everything and the slow painful building of a new structure, Hanna Page Antiques.

An awkward silence fell. The coffee was bitter, the cathedral bells were practice-ringing very loudly almost overhead, the young waitress was yawning. Doran gathered up her shoulder-bag.

"Thank you, that was lovely." It hadn't been, just sad. "I've got to go now. Look, do come and see me if you want any help or—or anything. Have you got a trade card?"

"Only an old one, from the place I've given up. I wouldn't like you to write there."

"All right. Here's mine. As to that figurine, don't worry, it'll sell, everything does. It's pretty and the sort of thing a lot of people collect, without bothering too much about authenticity."

Their parting was slightly uncomfortable, two people going their separate ways who had hoped for something better from the meeting. But what? A bargain, a find—an introduction, a footing in the district? Doran was not sure. She went out with Hanna to her car, still safe in the restaurant's park. It was a small Nissan of a conspicuous Mediterranean blue: not, thought Doran, a typical dealer's car.

"You'll find furniture a tight fit in that," she said.

"Oh. Yes, I shall, shan't I? Though actually I was thinking of sticking to small . . . accessibles."

"Collectables," Doran suggested.

"Yes, of course, collectables. How silly of me." She laughed. "Drunk again. I suppose I ought to get a bigger car, but I do love my little Bluebird. Well, goodbye. Lovely to have met you."

Doran was glad to be alone again, hugging her thoughts of home without the guilt-producing sight of someone else's deprivation. She window-shopped, bought some cream cheese from a delicatessen and a wooden toy that jerked its arms and legs when one pulled a string, walked in the cloisters and sat quietly among the noisy chattering tourist crowds in the cathedral.

It seemed more important than usual to get back to Christopher. He was well attended, Carole in charge, Vi working until four o'clock, Rodney at home. But she wanted to see him, to know that the bright image she had been displaying like a good hand of cards was real. Poor Hanna Page. It was to be hoped she was not familiar with Lamb's poignant *Dream Children.* "We are nothing; less

64

than nothing, and dreams. We are only what might have been . . ."

Doran drove a little faster than usual on the section of motorway which linked Barminster and Abbotsbourne.

Rodney pushed up his spectacles and rubbed his eyes. The dining room table was covered with books, his own and the library's, which contained information about local churches. He was compiling a list of the ones he must visit, with details of anything strange, beautiful or curious about them.

"Ecclesiology," he told Christopher, who was in his play-pen by the window, crawling rapidly from side to side in case he could find a point of exit. "The study of churches. I recommend it, my dear fellow, as being much easier and pleasanter than parish work. Not, mind you, that I don't feel an odd affection, almost nostalgia, for the old days back at that draughty, damp barn of a vicarage, having to keep un-civilized hours and being interminably helpful to people. In between pining for your mother. Ah me, I was a pale young curate then. Or if not exactly pale, or young, or a curate, I was a fair old mess. And look at me now."

Christopher looked at his father. His eyes filled with tears, his mouth became a perfect square, and he began to yell in his peculiarly penetrating voice.

"Now, now. There, there, hush." He scooped Christopher up and carried him to the table. "Look at the pretty churches, do. St. Eanswythe's, that's nice—or it was, until they gutted it and turned it into a Youth Centre. St. Alphege's: oh dear, that's a Culture Centre. But kindly ob-serve the Norman doorway, unequalled, I believe . . . Child, do stop. All right, I'll hand you over to Carole."

As he opened the door raised voices came to him from the kitchen opposite.

"I never did, I tell you." This was Carole.

"I saw you, didn't I? With my own eyes, plain as plain." Vi, furious.

"Tidying, that's all I was doing."

"Yes, and slipping things into your pocket, you dirty little sneakthief."

Carole began to whine. Christopher, aware of rivalry, stopped howling to listen.

"That's right, cry away," said Vi savagely. "That's all you can do, isn't it? You should think yourself lucky, my girl, a good place with good people like them to work for, and a lovely little boy that's no trouble—and soon as their back's turned you rob them right and left."

"Prove it, you old slag!"

"I would, and glad to, if you hadn't stuck it down your bra. Can't very well search you, can I, but I'm going to ring up Glen this minute and ask him to take you away and . . ."

A clamour broke out which sounded to Rodney like the accompaniment to some physical onslaught. With relief he heard Doran's voice. She always brought Helena home from school by the back door because a ramp had been made up the step for her wheelchair.

"What on earth's this?" Doran was saying. "Stop it at once. Vi, what's going on?"

Rodney quietly went back into the dining room and put Christopher back in the playpen. There, impressed, perhaps by the noise adults could make, he quietly began to eat a rag-book of nursery rhymes. Rodney thankfully went back to his churches.

When Doran appeared he swiftly went to her and kissed her, as he always did after they had been parted. Her cheeks were flushed.

"Trouble?"

"You heard all that?"

"It was fairly audible, yes."

Doran sat down. "I've never seen anything like it. Vi and Carole going at each other hammer and tongs like a couple of Furies. It seems Vi went in and caught Carole taking a fiver out of the cash I leave for the milkman and anyone like that who comes to the back door."

"And had she?"

"I rather think she had. I've thought once or twice that

66

it had gone down rather quickly, and—one or two other things. My best scent, for one. Of course she denied it hotly, and then she flounced out, saying she wasn't coming back. Oh dear."

Vi appeared at the door, with her coat on. Her high cheekbones flew crimson banners and her dark hair was dishevelled.

"I'm going now, Miss Doran." She was panting slightly. "And I think I ought to say I shall be glad to see the back of that little trollop. Sorry to have spoken out, and I hope it didn't disturb you, Mr. Rodney, but it was time somebody said something, after all she's got away with. It's my view she should never have come into this house, what with cheeking you in that sullen sort of way she has and the nasty manner I've heard her speak to Christopher when she thought nobody was listening, and taking toys he's been given for when he's older, and I for one shall be glad to see the back . . ."

Rodney foresaw the whole tirade about to be repeated and saw, also, that Doran was upset. He took command.

"All right, Vi. I think we both know how you feel. Shall we leave things to simmer down for the moment? Second thoughts, the still small voice of calm?"

Vi did not smile back.

Doran shivered. "There's never been such an outbreak of—wrath—in this house, since I've been here. I don't like it."

"Never mind, my darling. What's the matter—has something else happened?"

"No. No. I met a woman . . . I'll tell you later."

But perhaps she would not.

She picked up Christopher and held him so tightly that he protested, then playfully wound a fist in her hair and tugged. Acutely painful though it was, she unclasped his fingers very gently, and smiled on him.

Carole stayed away for two days, then reappeared at her usual time, very quiet and sulky. Doran said nothing about the whole affair. If the girl had taken the fiver, it was spent by now, and to raise the matter again would do no good. "We can't do without her, so we must simply put up with her," she said to Rodney, who agreed. He had never cared for Carole, but she was a necessary evil and part of the price they paid for having Christopher.

Vi refused to speak to Carole when their paths crossed, only sniffed and tossed her head. Helena was openly antagonistic: Vi had unwisely told her about the fracas.

"I don't think you ought to keep her, Doran. We know she's a thief, and I wouldn't be surprised if she was cruel to Christopher in a quiet way. He can't tell us himself, poor little boy—but she says nasty things to him, things Vi's overheard. Did you know she once called him a little bastard?"

"No, I didn't. Well, I don't like that at all, but I can't very well accuse her of it without having heard it myself, can I? And Christopher doesn't understand words like that yet. I'm sure she wouldn't actually ill-treat him, with children of her own at home. Anyway, I can't sack her, there's nobody else suitable round here. Let's just make the best of it."

"I hate her," Helena said. "I can't help it, I absolutely hate her. Utterly. Hate her, hate her, hate her. She's rotten to my brother and she robs you and Daddy." She wore a thundercloud face.

Oh dear: Annabella, come back, Doran thought. But Annabella was working hard for her A levels, and unavailable for counselling her friend.

Bell House had become a place of angry passions. "All we need is the Queen of Hearts," Rodney said as Doran was tucking Christopher up in his cot. He looked down into the Carroll showcase. "She isn't even here, in this little world, in a furious passion and shouting 'Off with his head!' Not a popular figure with modellers, I suppose. Don't look so worried, love, it will all pass."

"I hope so . . . We shall need Carole tomorrow, anyway."

Rodney had been invited to an afternoon meeting at Radio Dela, followed by drinks and refreshments, to which Doran was also asked.

"Vetting the wife," she said. "Always done in the best business circles, to make sure they won't disgrace you."

"Not RD's style at all. Not a glittering panoply of talent. Wait till you see it."

The exterior of Radio Dela was certainly not suggestive of glitter. An undistinguished building with new bits added on to a late nineteenth-century furniture repository, it was in the industrial outcrop of Eastgate. It had been set up there after starting life in a Queen Anne manor house behind Deal, but that charming seaside town had proved to be convenient for nobody, on the way to nowhere, and only the radio station's anagrammatic name remained of its birthplace. Rodney had told her that the old name of the town was Dole, according to Camden, but the governing body had felt this to be too downbeat to ensure the station's survival.

She was directed upstairs by the friendly young telephonist-cum-receptionist. Through the double swinging doors of the big studio the party was audible, but not to the usual volume. Not enough people? not enough drink? She pushed the doors open.

"Mrs. Chelmarsh? Of course. Hello." A bright-smiling young woman ticked her name off the list. Other young women surged about, denim-suited. Doran guessed that they would be called Mandy, Nicola, Kate, Penny, Victoria, that sort of thing. They were: she found it impossible to distinguish them, and gave up trying.

One of the nymphs offered her wine on a tray. Plonk, as usual. She accepted white, and a niblet of something fishy with pastry round it.

Across the room was Rodney, a cheering sight among strangers. His eyes lit up at the sight of her, and he waved, and spoke to an extremely tall young woman who turned out to be Public Relations, and called Penelope.

Penelope conducted Doran to a craggy-faced shortish man who yet contrived to be conspicuous. His movements were swiftly rotatory, windmill-like, between one person and another. Wild and whirling words, thought Doran. He flashed irregular teeth in a social smile, he clapped men on

69

the shoulder and swept women into an embrace, and all the time he talked.

"Our Station Manager, Jim Fontenoy," said Penelope. "Doran Chelmarsh."

Fontenoy stopped whirling, fixed Doran with an intent stare, and clasped her hand in both of his.

"Of course, of course. But I know you. I've heard so much." The grip tightened and Doran winced.

"I don't think . . ," she began.

"Yes," he went on rapidly. "Not really Chelmarsh. Fairweather. Queen of the wonderful world of antiques. Brilliant mind. Flawless taste. A perfect woman, nobly planned. Invite me."

"I'm sorry . . .?"

"I shall call on you. At home. Soon."

He fixed her with what she would have thought of as a glittering eye if there hadn't been enough clichés in the air already.

"We shall be delighted to see you," she replied firmly, "but do telephone first. I'm at the shop nearly every day and Rodney will be away a lot, and with a young baby in the house . . ."

"Yes, yes, yes." With one final squeeze of her hand he moved on to the next person.

Still nursing her fingers, Doran was reclaimed by Penelope.

"Is he always like that?" Doran asked.

"Always like what?"

"Well. Intense. Overwhelming."

"Dunno. I've only just taken over. He talks a lot. Come and meet the local lord. Got a castle in a park, stinking rich, unlike most of 'em."

The local lord made no claim to previous acquaintance with Doran and showed no desire to cultivate her. Penelope steered him away, leaving Doran gazing hopefully round the studio.

There was one familiar face, Barton Boswell, an actor she remembered hero-worshipping when he had toured Ox-

70

ford in her youth. He was old and beaky now, vague and pathetic, but she still remembered his magic.

"I used to adore you, Mr. Boswell," she said, emboldened by two glasses of really rather nasty wine.

"Did you, child? How lovely. I wish I'd known."

"In fact, you did. I used to hang round the stage door and try to touch you."

"Ah." He sighed deeply. "Like to try it now?"

She put a hand on his, dry and papery, spotted with age. He smiled and laid a light kiss on her cheek. "Bless you."

A large woman in red, far larger than she ought to have been, turned out aptly to be a financial bulwark of the company. She was loud and cheerful and quite well informed.

"Churches, Tessa told me. You get your husband round to ours, sweet little place, you'd love it, so would he— thirteenth-century glass, brass memorial to a falconer, one to a lady called Charitye."

"Thank you. I'll tell him. He'd enjoy that sort of thing."

"Delicious, isn't he? I could take him home with me, I must say."

Like hell you will. Doran moved swiftly to the most attractive man within her reach and addressed him without an introduction.

"Hello. I'm Doran Fairweather. I mean Chelmarsh."

The dark eyes glowed at her. The face was olive-skinned, exotic—French, Italian? Hard to tell. Not particularly tall. But very good-looking. Somewhere in the thirties. Expression melancholy in repose. But the full mouth had a smile for her—for any pretty woman, she guessed.

"Hello. Jacob Fraser."

"Doran Chelmarsh. Or Fairweather, depending!" Jewish, then, with a forename like Jacob, though the Fraser was odd, but there had once been a quaint custom which bobbed up in old novels of Jews calling themselves Macsporran and the like. Jacob Fraser didn't look as if he had ever called himself Macsporran. He was extremely well dressed in clothes which managed to be afternoon-casual without overdoing it.

"Depending on what?" he asked. She told him at length,

amazed by her own loquacity, as the deer-like eyes dwelt on hers. He was a very ready listener. She found herself talking about trade, about her life, about Christopher, about Abbotsbourne. Suddenly she realized how impolite she was being to monopolize the conversation.

"Are you Dela staff?" she asked.

"No. Just an interested party."

"A programme contributor, like my husband? He's doing a series on local churches."

A shake of the head. His hair, sweeping over his brow in a curve, was like a raven's wing, Doran thought unoriginally. Someone came up and annexed him, to her disappointment, and she moved on, nursing her glass, to question Penelope.

"Fraser?" The PR girl paused in mid-scurry. "New backer, pots of money, I believe. Nick over there knows more, ask him."

Nick over there was another familiar face, from a year and a bit ago: a radio presenter who had been recording at Caxton Manor's Antiques Roadshow. She had always remembered that gothic face—Lancelot, perhaps, after the Guinevere affaire had burnt itself out. There was wit and disillusion there and, with a pang, she registered silvered hair and brown sherry eyes like Henry Gore, once loved and twice lost.

There is no armour against certain spells. After an opportunity once missed, it seemed a pity not to seize this one. With the purest of intentions, Doran very much wanted to hear that beautiful, warm, slightly edged voice again. She set off in his direction.

With that mysterious radar which operates between couples who know each other intimately, she was halted by the knowledge that Rodney wanted to attract her attention. Even across the room his face told her that he knew exactly what she was meditating.

She changed direction, meeting him halfway.

"Good," he said. "Come on, we're leaving."

"Why?"

"Because Jim's just going to make his speech. We've

72

had it once already at the meeting, and he goes on and on—then, then, methinks, how sweetly flows the liquefaction of his prose. This is the New Age of radio, we here at Dela are marching as to war against our hated rivals we-don't-name-names-but, it's not technology alone that wins though we've plenty of that, it's vitality, enthusiasm, a fresh approach . . ."

By this time they were at the double doors. Doran cast a wistful look behind her. Perhaps she was doomed, like the Lady of Shalott, never to meet Sir Lancelot face to face. Jim Fontenoy was standing on a chair (necessary with his lack of inches).

With sudden discomfort she realized that he was looking straight at her across the heads of the company. She tried to remember what Rodney had told her about him. That he was particularly interested in her? That he had asked questions? Why?

"Why is your boss staring?" she hissed at Rodney.

"Staring? Is he? I think he's just catching eyes. He likes an attentive audience. Ssh, he's off. Head for that door, quick. Let us softly and suddenly vanish away."

That was what the Snark's victims had done when it proved to be a Boojum. But Jim Fontenoy was nothing like the nightmare monster which Carroll himself had found "quite unimaginable".

Or was he?

Quite steady on what looked like a very unreliable rostrum, he was beaming from side to side. Doran heard the phrases "New Age of radio . . . marching as to war, no doubt you'll recognize the quotation, certainly our friend the Reverend Rodney will, ha ha . . . not technology alone. . . ." They crept out.

On the drive home they chatted desultorily. Rodney was looking forward to his new assignment. He had been warned, he said, to be strictly lay in his approach to his chosen churches—no bias, no vicar stuff, no moralizing.

"As if I would. I shall be as splendidly detached as a . . . what's splendidly detached?"

"Look out," Doran warned. Rain was falling, making the

73

road surface slippery and the visibility poor as they approached the double carriageway which led to the valley. "There's a lot of traffic for this time of the evening. Oh lord, an accident."

Ahead of them, an ambulance, a police car and a knot of people were gathered round a vehicle they could not see.

"I'd better stop," Rodney said. "Not ghoulishness. You know."

Doran knew. He was used to being summoned to accidents in case the sort of comfort he could dispense might be required. He pulled in behind the ambulance, and got out. Doran followed him.

"There might be something I could do," she said, to her own surprise.

The crashed car had rocked on to its side, its boot and rear bumpers badly dented. It was a blue Nissan, Doran noticed: she was not usually observant about makes of cars but she had, surely, seen one recently.

Two ambulance men, with police standing by, were tending someone lying on a red blanket. The police viewed Rodney's approach without favour.

"I'm a priest," he said. "C of E. Ex-St. Crispin's, Abbotsbourne. I thought perhaps one of my—neighbours might be involved."

"Have a look, sir," said the elder policeman. "But if it's nobody you know we'd rather you didn't stay—it only encourages gawpers."

"Of course." He surveyed the woman on the ground. She was unknown to him, and was obviously beyond his help, or anybody's. He touched the little crucifix that always hung round his neck, and was about to turn away when Doran clutched at his arm.

"Wait! It's somebody I know."

"Yes, madam?" Both policemen brightened up.

"At least—I've met her. How extraordinary. Her name's Hanna Page."

Chapter 6

A Bandersnatch
swiftly drew nigh

Rodney was familiar with Eastgate nick, from a previous occasion. It looked to him like any other police station, apart from being much larger than the ones he and Doran had visited during their Cotswold adventure. People seemed to be typing, using word processors, or telephoning in every square inch of it. But one well-known face materialized before them: Sam Eastry, once community constable of Abbotsbourne, now translated to this higher sphere.

Fatherly, protective, he drew Rodney and Doran out of the babel into a glassed-off partition with a desk in it.

"My little corner. I'll get another chair. There. Now tell me all."

Middle-aged, plump, gently moustached, he was the very image of a benevolent police officer. He smoked a pipe at home, but not on duty. He had been a father figure to Doran for years. She was wholly comfortable in his presence.

Doran told him all, such as it was. The telephone call inviting her to lunch in Barminster, the lunch itself and everything she could remember about Hanna Page. Sam jotted down notes, unostentatiously.

"That's absolutely the lot," she finished. "We parted after lunch, and she didn't get in touch again, though I thought she might. She hadn't a trade card and she didn't volunteer an address."

"The lady didn't volunteer much, it seems," said Sam. "Including the fact that her real name was Hanna Moreton and she was an actress with a flat in London—Bayswater—

and no connection with Cheshire so far as we can trace. Or, Doran, with the antiques trade."

Doran gasped. "But . . . she seemed to know such a lot." She paused. Sam's steady gaze was like a doctor's, aware that his patient has more symptoms than she has admitted to, and willing her to utter them.

"No. You're right, Sam. She didn't know much. How to unwrap a fragile piece of porcelain without covering the place with bits of paper. Anything about Samson of Paris, though I think she did know the figure was a fake—but not why. She even got the word collectables wrong. I thought that was funny at the time, but then the wine might have affected her memory. And she had the wrong sort of car. She was a fake herself."

"If I might make an inference," Rodney said, "she could have been set up."

"Vinadas," said Doran.

"Possibly." They told Sam about Vinadas. By this time a young man had appeared beside him and was taking notes. Doran remembered the new police evidence-recording procedure. Sam was obviously sparing them anything so alarming. The young policeman went off to make checks and telephone calls, Sam behind him.

"You didn't tell me about these uncertainties of yours," Rodney said.

"Well, no. I suppose I felt a trifle strange about the whole thing. Something to do with Christopher, I think. I felt so sorry for her because . . . good heavens."

When Sam came back they were gazing at four small photographs ranged on the desk. Doran pointed to them.

"It couldn't be anything to do with those? Oh, I do hope not. I showed them to her—I don't remember whether she specifically asked to see them, but I'd have shown them to her anyway. You know how it is, Sam."

Sam said that he knew how it was. His own wallet contained at least ten pictures of his Jennifer. He examined the photographs carefully, then selected the one taken with a flash in the nursery.

"I think that might well have been what Mrs. Page or

Moreton wanted to see." Christopher, laughing in his cot: the Lewis Carroll showcase behind him indistinguishable in detail, its glaze a dazzle of brilliance from the flash. On the wall above it, the cherub showing clear and three-dimensional. The gift on the scrolls was highlighted. The blood drops shone like holly berries.

Doran said nothing. Rodney put his hand over hers.

"You've got a hot property there, Doran," Sam said. "Not hot in the trade sense—dangerous. The old chap, Vinadas, wanted it very badly, you say. Badly enough to put her on to you, and find out where it was in the house, and then kill her?"

Doran shook her head. "How do I know? I shouldn't have thought so. He seemed a bit mad, but murder—why? He could just have paid her . . ."

"You say murder. Interesting." Sam had been studying notes put before him by his silent young aide. "I didn't mention murder to you before, did I? But from the preliminary medical examination it seems that she died from a blow on the back of the head, somewhere not too far from the medulla oblongata. Doesn't need an autopsy to find that out. Somebody ran her car off the road, then opened the driver's door and coshed her while she was still shocked. She fell forward against the steering wheel, but that only caused light bruising to the face."

"Murder," said Doran. "I knew it was, when I saw her there on the road. Because of me."

"Not because of you," Rodney said gently. "Because of that carving on the wall. Vinadas cursed you for not giving it to him, remember? Anyone who'd lay a curse might be capable of killing. You must get rid of it. I know you like it, it means a lot to you, but it mustn't stay there after this. You've had one unsuccessful burglary already. You do see, Doran?"

She saw: Christopher's sleeping face, the cherub hanging over him like a Damoclean sword, Vinadas somehow appearing between the window curtains like a white-faced, white-haired ghost in an old pier-end peepshow. There was one at Brighton. There were several at Madame Tussaud's. Threatening, goblin faces.

"All right. I don't want it now, after what's happened. Only we can't get it down by ourselves, can we, Rodney?"

"I shouldn't care to try. Our own feeble efforts were so inept that we got a pal of Howell's to come and do it, with Rawlplugs and things we don't even know the name for. Including a false back, metal with those rings all round the edge."

"Len would that be?" Sam asked. "Freelance builder, big chap with a Belfast accent?"

"That's him," Doran said. "Rough but reliable."

"He worked here for a bit last year. Can you get him to do it tonight, when you get home?"

Doran looked taken aback. "Well, no. I don't know where he lives, and I do know he hasn't got a car—it would mean taking him to Abbotsbourne and driving him home afterwards, and Rodney's got to take Carole home as well . . ." She looked at her watch. "We're late as it is."

"And," said Rodney, "something tells me that by this time in the evening Len will have a few jars taken. He likes his drop, does Len."

"Besides," Doran added, "it would disturb Christopher, so long after his bedtime, wouldn't it? No, it will have to wait till tomorrow."

Sam ruffled his hair and frowned. "Well, I don't like it, but I suppose there's not much we can do—unless you'd like us to send someone to do the job."

"No," said Doran firmly. "We've had enough happening today. One more night won't make any difference. We must go, Sam, if you don't want us any more."

"There's just one thing." Sam was looking at the notes before him. "One of the ambulance men heard Mrs. Page or Moreton whisper something just before she died, which was very soon after they got to her. Almost reflex-action speech, I imagine, she shouldn't have been capable of saying anything by then, but these things happen. He thought she said, 'James, no.' "

They were in bed at last, drinking a nightcap of very hot

78

whisky and water. The night was warm, but only a strong hot drink seemed adequate. The bedroom door was open, and the nursery door. Doran had avoided glancing at the cherub as she had checked the peacefully sleeping Christopher.

"I suppose it's occurred to you," she said, "that Vinadas's name wasn't James. It was Paul."

"So he said. But perhaps it wasn't really Vinadas either. In which case the police will have their work cut out to trace him. I suppose his contacts would be the best source—museum people, collectors. Oh, I don't know." He blinked wearily. "I think we'd better go to sleep now, if you've got to be at Eastgate early, Len-hunting."

He had almost drifted into sleep when Doran spoke again.

"Darling. Sorry. But it's worrying me. Do you know anything about Jim Fontenoy?"

Rodney was divided between amusement and irritation. "Oh, Doran. Remember what curiosity did for the cat Pensive Selima? And no, I don't know a lot about Jim, and what I do know can keep till morning." He turned away from her.

Doran lay staring towards the invisible canopy of their four-poster. Jim. James, no. The poor thing's last words a protest against the hand that was to strike her death blow. Someone had struck Doran like that, once, but she had survived. Hanna had not.

I was so sorry for her. Surely she wasn't pretending grief for her childlessness, even if she was an actress.

I shall call on you, at home, soon. Who had said that? Jim Fontenoy. James.

Doran was not over-happy about asking Carole to spend another day in charge of Christopher. Both Vi and Helena had been very vehement against the girl. But at the worst she had only spoken nastily to him, not ill-treated him, and if she did nick the odd toy for her own children she ought to be charitable about it, their need being greater than Christopher's, presumably. Anyway, it wouldn't be for long.

And soon they would seriously try to find a replacement for Carole, if it could be done without breaking the bank. How wonderful if they could have had Tiggy Denshaw ...

Carole was not pleased to be asked. Doran had stopped to collect her after taking Helena to school. After, because Helena still refused to speak to her.

"Here all yesterday evening, wasn't I, and much later than you said. I've got kids as well, you know, it's not fair on my Trev having to stay in with 'em, and come home in his lunchtime as well, now is it?"

"No, well, I'm sorry. But I didn't know I'd have to go to Eastgate today. In fact it's a sort of emergency. Vi's working somewhere else, so I'm afraid I'll just have to ask you, Carole." Doran weakened, though she knew it was a mistake. "I'll pay you extra, and there's a chicken casserole in the fridge."

"Oh, all right." Carole had turned the process of giving in with a bad grace into a fine art. Doran gave Christopher his bath, talked to him, gave instructions that he was to be put in the garden. It was a beautiful morning, pale gold light and the promise of hot sunshine later. Rodney decided that he might as well keep an appointment at a church west of Barminster, which was normally locked and was being opened for his inspection by special agreement.

"I'll probably be back for lunch," Doran told Carole. "It depends how quickly I can find the person I'm going to look for. Oh, and will you make sure we've got eggs and bacon? And beer."

Len would certainly expect lavish food. When he had put up the carving he had eaten three fried eggs, bacon, beans and left-over potatoes, and half a large fruit pie. Doran wondered whether it would be too expensive to send him down to the Rose. Yes, she decided, it would, and he would almost certainly talk about the reason for his being at Bell House. The less said about that the better.

"And you're sure you won't change your mind and decide to keep the thing, after all?" Rodney asked. "We know what a difference the light of day makes. But I do hope you won't."

"I won't. It's gone, whatever magic it had for me. Truly. And they're sending a police car for it, so that we won't have to risk anything by keeping it on the premises. Oh, and I've asked Christopher whether he'll miss it, and he says he won't, he'd rather have that ghastly Disneyfied rabbit with fluorescent fur that Vi gave him."

"Good. Excellent judgement on his part. Take care. Don't let Len smoke those vulture's-nest fags in the nursery." He kissed her, at length. She was looking fragile this morning, an appearance which brought his protective instincts rushing to the fore.

His car was gone, out of sight up Mays Lane. They had each kept their cars after their marriage: not an extravagance but a necessity, since both were needed professionally.

Howell was not yet at the shop, having spent an evening which had left him somewhat thick in the head.

"Len? No, I don't know where he lives. Not his keeper, am I?"

"No, but you must have some idea—he's worked here a lot on odd jobs."

Howell gulped strong tea. "Honest, I haven't, not a bloody clue. At a guess it'd be somewhere down near the station."

"Oh dear. What's his other name, then?—I know it's something unusual."

Howell looked dazed, as though the black smoke rising from the electric toaster were fogging his brain.

"Look, you want to know too much, *merch*, this time of a morning. How do I . . . Yes, I do. Wood. Or is it Woods?"

Doran persisted. No, Howell had not seen Len for a week or two. He would be hard to find, since he worked for most of the building firms in the town. He held a union card and was free to go where he liked, as the fancy took him. Could even be working for a private employer, outside Eastgate.

Doran waited for Howell to finish his breakfast, persuaded him that he could perfectly well shave at the shop, and drove him there, grumbling. She was not going to tell him about the imminent departure of the cherub: it might start something, excite Arthur Hidley into making another vicarious bid. It was merely a tricky carpentering job she wanted doing at home, she said.

She was resigned to a long search. It was so important that the man who had put the cherub up so ingeniously should also take it down: and important not to have a completely unknown workman in the nursery. Armed with a list of names of local firms of builders, culled from the Yellow Pages, she settled herself at the telephone and rang them, one by one. It was an unsatisfactory business. A very young female voice, who sounded as if it were her first day on duty, would answer, eventually. She didn't know who was working for them at the moment. She'd ask, if the caller would hang on. Sometimes her voice would go away and never return, lost in the air-waves.

Or a man would answer, and say that he had no idea, he would pass her on to the gaffer, who was on the other phone. The gaffer would never have heard of a Len Wood or Woods. And so it went on.

Doran grew desperate. The minutes were ticking on. It was now late morning. At last, frustrated and annoyed, she slammed the receiver down and went for an unsatisfactory drive round the district, stopping whenever she saw work in progress on building sites. Out to the suburbs, down to the harbour, along the railway where some old sheds were being demolished, she asked for Len in vain. Nobody owned to having heard of him, and she was the butt of a good many rude, suggestive remarks.

Mad ideas flitted through hr mind about the Hunting of the Snark. They sought it with thimbles, they sought it with care. They pursued it with forks and hope; They threatened its life with a railway-share, They charmed it with smiles and soap.

All very ingenious, she thought grimly, if you were conducting a search in some fantastic country of the mind, as Lewis Carroll was. Great fun. If you were in the real world and trying to find a man to do a necessary and urgent job, not so amusing.

She drove to the police station, parking in the last few inches of space left in the VISITORS ON OFFICIAL BUSINESS ONLY section. Sam was out, but her old friend Detective-Inspector Burnelle was produced. He listened carefully, not interrupting, to what she had to say.

"You ought to be with us, you know, Mrs. Chelmarsh. Great command of facts, don't waste words. Well, I'd heard a bit of all this, about the attempted burglary—ever get your ring back, by the way?—but the rest of it's new to me. All right, we'll see what we can do."

Doran felt better. She liked Burnelle and knew that he admired her. She sat back in the visitors' chair, relaxing, until young WPC Jo Allison came over and made small talk about the weather, petrol prices and Rodney, who had, it seemed, made a deep impression on her.

"That's fixed, then," said Burnelle, returning. "PC Reed's the man for the job, and never mind your friend Len. He's strong and willing and quite a handyman."

If PC Reed was, indeed, as strong as he looked that was very strong indeed. He was no more than twenty-two, proportionately broad, fat in the face, and rather resembled a remarkably portly baby boy whom Doran often saw at the Infants' Clinic, only Christopher's age but twice his size. Reed, whose name turned out to be Desmond, proved to be a pleasant lad, with, he admitted modestly, an O level in carpentry.

He followed Doran to Abbotsbourne in his panda. He could double as remover of the cherub from the wall and from the premises: it had really turned out very conveniently.

There was no sign of Carole in the front garden, or, as they passed through it on their way to the kitchen door, at the back. And no sign of lunch on the table. Carole had evidently decided that the midday sun was too hot for Christopher. Though it was a wonder that she was not sunbathing and Christopher put out under a tree. Carole was avid for sun, not that it did anything for her complexion.

Desmond Reed was gazing round with admiration.

"Lovely house you've got here. Not many like this. I like old antiques, myself."

"So do I. I really ought to sell some of these, when I can bear to part with them. Would you like to take your tie off? It's terribly close in here. The nursery's upstairs, if you'll follow me."

He followed her with his bag of tools, not too fast because he was trying to take in the pictures on the staircase. It was like visiting an art gallery or a stately home open to the public, this job. And a pretty girl to show him round. He hoped the other girl, the nanny or whatever, would be pretty too. Hot weather made him feel like that.

"Carole! I'm back. Where are you?"

Reaching the top of the stairs, Doran saw that the nursery door was open.

"Carole?"

She was there, between the nursery door and the window, lying on her face. A lot of blood had got on to the cream vinyl flooring. She was still and silent: not breathing.

The cot was empty.

Afterwards Doran would remember Reed saying, "Christ!" and herself throwing open door after door and shouting, and Reed telling her to take it easy. She thought he telephoned at one point. She ran downstairs and out into the garden and back into the house, looking under furniture, turning over cushions, opening cupboards, wildly calling Christopher's name, as though he could have answered even if he had been there.

Then she fell over something, or blacked out, and strong hands lifted her. She found herself lying in one of the drawing room armchairs, Richenda Berg from next door looking anxiously down at her. Richenda was wearing a black bikini and most of her was toast-brown.

"Doran," she was saying, "Doran. Come on now, drink this."

Brandy was what fainting people were supposed to get, but Richenda had poured from the first bottle she could see, which was a bottle of gin. The taste was so nasty that Doran shook her head, spluttered and sat up.

"That's better," Richenda said. "Are you back with us?"

Doran nodded.

"I heard you yelling and hopped the fence. Your policeman friend's told me what happened. God, what a thing."

"Put my coat on," Doran said helpfully, "you'll get cold."

"No, I won't. Just keep quiet, you're not making sense. The kettle should have boiled by now—I expect the boy's seeing to it. Oh good, here he is." Desmond had appeared at the door with a tray most professionally laid. Looking monumentally calm, he poured tea for the three of them. It was hot and very strong, a man's brew.

"Rodney. I want Rodney," Doran said.

"Yes. Where is he?" asked Richenda.

"Gone to look at a church, madam," volunteered Desmond, "other side of Barminster, Mrs. Chelmarsh told me earlier. Shouldn't be late, she said."

The tea was extraordinarily restorative. Doran pulled herself together.

"I'm sorry," she said. "I must have gone mad for the moment. But Christopher wasn't there. You haven't found him, have you?" She was afraid of the answer.

But Desmond said, "No, madam. He's been lifted, it seems. No sign anywhere, and I've looked, I can tell you. But don't worry, I've put it in hand." Doran could almost have smiled at being told not to worry. She noticed Richenda's furrowed brow, the absence of that air of queenliness and coquetry she usually wore, a blend of Garbo and Monroe. A nice, available man sat only a yard from her, a somewhat sweaty and overblown young buddha, but quite personable, yet she was not even looking at him, only at Doran.

Desmond was saying that he had telephoned Eastgate as soon as he had made sure that the baby was not in the house or garden, and that there were signs of a hurried exit by somebody. He had also telephoned for an ambulance.

"The young woman had some life in her, blood was still running and I could feel a slight pulse. I did what I could to make her comfortable. I think she's got a chance."

"Did you ask her about Christopher? What did she say?" Doran demanded feverishly.

"Oh, she wasn't in any state to talk, madam, not at all. They'd nearly finished her off, only she was lucky." He longed to describe his patient's exact injury, a vicious stabwound which he guessed had penetrated the left lung, the first aid he had given, his views on the method of attack, all the knowledge so carefully hoarded from his training course days. But a tact rare in one so young and inexperienced kept him from saying any more, merely that he had also telephoned the community constable who was coming straight over.

"And there's something I think you ought to see," he added. "In the ... where the young woman is."

Richenda and Doran followed him upstairs. On the floor of the nursery Carole had been turned over, straightened out and covered with blankets tucked up round her ears. Her face was a dreadful colour: Doran thought horribly of some corpse in a ballad warning somebody else not to kiss their clay-cold lips. It was hard to believe that Carole could be alive.

"Up there." Desmond pointed to the wall opposite the door. The cherub was still there, but it hung askew, the wallpaper round it torn, lumps of plaster on the floor, dislodged by somebody's frantic attempts to detach the carving. Part of the scroll bordering the cherub's figure had been broken off. But Len's master-hand had been too much for a thief obviously not armed with the right tools. A bloodstained screwdriver—not belonging to the house—lay broken, a wedge sometimes used to prop open a window had been used to force the carving away from the wall, and had splintered.

"Botched job," said Desmond. The shriek of an ambulance siren came from the distance towards them and stopped at the front gate.

Rodney had had a good day with his notebook and camera. He had collected the memorial brass of a lady called Esperaunce, a set of the Seven Deadly Sins in stone, carved with startling realism, a rare piscina and two epitaphs which had somehow passed the local censor. Witty phrases sparkled through his mind as he opened the drawing room door.

"I'm back," he called carefully. "Late, late in the gloaming Kilmeny came home, with an appetite quite unlike ..."

The talking halted: the faces turned towards him. Doran, looking ill, Richenda, Vi, Reed, Glen Lidell and his wife Kate, and Sam Eastry.

He drew a deep breath, and waited for them to tell him what had happened.

Chapter 7

Baby into Pig

"So there's no more to be done," Doran said with frozen calm, "but wait."

It was nine o'clock in the evening. Of those who had been there when Rodney returned, only Richenda and Sam were left, and Constable Reed up in the nursery. He had, with fearful noise, removed the cherub from the wall, and stayed on guard in case another attempt were made on it.

He had come down and reported, ruefully, the state of mess his operations had caused. "I'm afraid you'll have to have the wall re-plastered and decorated. Whoever put that thing up meant it to stay. Perhaps you'd like to come and see."

Doran said that she would not, on the whole, bother. To enter the empty nursery was something she preferred not to face. Richenda thought that both parents looked like people waiting in a cell for Revolutionary guards to summon them to the guillotine.

Helena had gone into severe shock when told of her brother's disappearance and seemed so ill that Nurse Kate had been sent for. She had given the patient a strong sedative and stayed with her until sleep took over.

They had not intended to tell Helena about the attack on Carole, but she had asked questions. At the answer, all her old malevolence came back, and more.

"I said so," she told Doran. "I said she wasn't fit to look after him. She called Vi names, but she was worse than any of them herself. She was a liar and she stole from you, and she was jealous of Christopher's clothes and toys. Will she die?"

"Oh, Helena, nobody knows. They'll do their best at the hospital, but she was very badly hurt."

"Good. I hope she dies. If Christopher isn't brought back, I hope she dies in agony. I wish I'd killed her myself."

Doran left the room without answering. Kate followed, her normally cheerful blunt-nosed face solemn.

"Is she usually delirious, Mrs. Chelmarsh, with a bad turn like this?"

"I've never seen her quite as—quite so disturbed. But then, things have never been so . . . serious."

"No. Well, I should let Dr. Fullathorn know if she gets worse. He might suggest . . ."

Committal, Kate thought, but kept the thought to herself. Committal to a psychiatric unit where a dangerous patient should be restrained. Kate was used to unpleasant behaviour from those she attended, but something about Helena troubled her more than usual. She remembered the little claws of hands, the vindictiveness in the voice. Surely the girl couldn't have got up the stairs in her wheelchair?

But if it had not been in her wheelchair. If she had heard the baby crying, and crawled up on all fours, as she could at a pinch? If the child had gone, taken by somebody else, and Carole was still there?

Kate realized that her imagination was becoming as fevered as the girl's. She was glad when Helena slept, and she could escape to the neat, safe, police house, and the messages on her answering machine, and Glen's supper.

"At least we're certain it's a kidnap." Sam was angry and weary, angry that what he considered the lowest and worst of crimes should have happened to the girl he thought of as his daughter, almost as Jennifer was and Jane had been. Also to his friend, the innocent unworldly Rodney. He wished he had never left Abbotsbourne: yet he wanted very much to be at home in Eastgate now, because he was forty-nine, and tired.

"The Yard's pulling out all the stoppers to trace Mr. Vinadas—no sign yet—and a general call's gone out for any child of the right age who's suddenly appeared in any household. Though that's usually applicable only in domestic kidnaps, women stealing babies for some reason. Reed and Glen have searched every inch of the gardens in Mays Lane—the light's gone now, that's it for the night. I'll get more men up in the morning, but that's all we can do for the moment."

"I don't see where else we could have looked," Doran said. "We've covered the district in cars, mine and Rodney's and Richenda's. We went right to the end of the estate, including the very new houses where people have only just moved in. We even drove round the backs and called at anywhere that had—babies' washing hanging out."

Rodney put his hand on hers. "It was a pity about the St. Crispin's Ladies' Outing, the Duttons taking a coachful of parishioners—including a lot who weren't—to Stoneley Castle. Lunch and sightseeing and a forty-mile drive each way. It was cheap, they couldn't resist. So they were all out, all the women who notice things, and nobody who was left saw anything unusual."

"It must have been a car," said Richenda, "I mean, a car that took Christopher. You can't just walk through the streets of a small place like this clutching a baby, especially a baby everybody knows. But nobody noticed a strange car. Of course, a car's not very remarkable, with so many trippers. You got nothing from the shopkeepers?"

"No, they weren't very cooperative." Sam was saddened by the number of small shops which had closed since his time in the village, giving way to emptiness or mini-markets. The Asian proprietors of these had been amiable and helpful, but could hardly be expected to take note of variations in the life of a community new to them.

Richenda went restlessly to the window and stared out into the summer dusk. A few lights sparkling in neighbours' houses, including one in her own kitchen, to foil anyone who might think the house was empty. The sound of a passing car.

She spun round suddenly, illuminating that dolorous room with hope. Once Rodney would have made amused comparisons with moments in the filmic lives of silent screen heroines, historic films being at the moment his hobby now that a video had joined the household. Richenda's silvery beauty and Slav bones would have enchanted D.W. Griffith. But such things were far from his mind as she spoke.

"I *did* see a car. At least a van. Outside your gate, late morning, or round noon. Yes, it must have been before noon. I was out at the front watering a young azalea before the sun got at it."

"What kind of van?" Doran's voice was eager for the first time.

"Well, that was the funny thing—it was a pork butcher's."

"Mr. Turner's?"

"Is that his name? The local one, anyway. I wouldn't have noticed it but I sort of thought pork wasn't exactly the ideal thing for this weather, unless you were having a Sunday roast anyway, or . . ."

"Actually," Doran said, "I don't awfully like eating pork, and Rodney humours me." He was glad of her smile. "Are you sure the van was at our gate?"

"Perfectly."

"Well, I haven't ordered any pork and Vi wouldn't without asking me. Could the van have broken down?"

"Could have." Richenda sounded dubious. "But there was nobody tinkering with it, and nobody in the driver's seat. Isn't it extraordinary how one remembers details, when one hadn't even noticed them at the time."

"Very," said Rodney. "Subconscious. We must go and interview Mr. Turner."

"At this time of night? He'll be closed."

"He lives in a detached cottage at the end of Church Path," Doran said. "And I don't care what time of night it is, personally. Sam, you'll come with us, won't you—we need authority and I should think it might be the only way to deal with Mr. Turner."

She was almost like herself now that there was something to do, Rodney thought, for as long as the stimulation lasted. He was trying not to clutch at hope, but he knew that she must if she were not to break.

Richenda volunteered to stay in the house. "Just in case the phone rings." They all knew what kind of call she meant. "And I could make Desmond another pot of tea, and tuck him up in his folding bed if he's sleepy." She giggled, and Rodney marvelled. It was the first time he had ever encountered his next-door neighbour in an unseductive mood; he found, to his surprise, that he had missed it.

Sam's presence proved to be essential in dealing with the pork butcher. Mr. Turner was displeased to be called upon at his home late at night. He refused at first to open the door, calling through the letter box that he didn't admit visitors after dark or charity collectors at any time.

"Police," Sam informed him. There was a silence on the other side of the door.

"Police, are you? Show me your credentials."

"Don't be silly, Jack. It's me, Sam."

Sam pushed his card through the letter box. After a moment, the door-chain was taken off and bolts drawn. When the door opened, J. S. Turner stood before them, still fully dressed. Sam was well known to him, but he glowered at them all. His drooping grey-black moustache did not do anything to enliven his expression.

Politely but firmly Sam ushered the other two into the small square hall, past the obstructive form of its owner. Television voices came through a closed door.

"I don't know what this is about . . ." Turner began predictably, to be interrupted by Doran.

"Our son's been kidnapped, Mr. Turner. Your van was seen outside our house about the time it must have happened."

Turner looked from one face to another, outraged.

"And what the hell's that got to do with me? Do you think *I* kidnapped your son, whoever he may be?"

"I think you know perfectly well," Rodney said. "My wife may not spend much time in your shop, but then you didn't spend much time in what was my church—we're still neighbours, not enemies. Come on."

"If you'd just answer one or two questions, Jack," Sam said. "We're sure it's nothing to do with you, but the van was seen and anything at all you can tell us may be extremely helpful. If we could come in, perhaps—?"

"All right." Turner went before them into the sitting room, where they heard him talking. He showed them, still unsmilingly, into it. By an electric log fire Mrs. Turner, a dumpy woman, and Arnold, the tall thin son of the Turners, were watching a television spectacular.

"Really, it's a bit late," Mrs. Turner said. "I do think . . ."

"I wanted to watch this," added Arnold for both of them. His father gave him a discouraging look.

"Perhaps the kitchen might be easier to talk in," Sam suggested.

In the kitchen, seated round the table, Rodney saw Doran's face grow haggard again, as Jack Turner told them that he had not taken his van out that day, that he and Arnold had been serving in the shop from nine in the morning until five in the afternoon, with three quarters of an hour's break at home for lunch. So there, his expression implied.

"Where was the van parked all this time?" Sam asked.

"You know bloody well where it was parked. Where it always is, outside the Rose, courtesy of Win Bellacre after you'd stuck your nose in and tried to get it shifted."

"Those spaces are supposed to be for Rose customers, not for trade vehicles," Sam replied mildly. "But it's the Bellacres' land and if they want to let you park there we can't stop them." The landlord and his wife were very good customers of Turner's, and a friendly relationship existed between them, he knew.

"What does it matter?" Doran almost shouted. "Who cares what his parking arrangements are? It's Christopher we're talking about."

"Is it there now?" Sam asked Turner.

"I suppose so. If it's not been pinched, as you seem to be suggesting, in which case it isn't. As you *are* here, and my peaceful evening's gone up the spout, we might as well go and look."

"If you don't mind." Turner went back into the sitting

room, where the television was still emitting shouts and screams, and returned to lead them out. Along Church Path and past the leaning gravestones, past the new, incongruous house where the Bruces lived he led them, going before them in sullen silence. Doran clung to Rodney's arm so tightly that he found it difficult to walk at his usual pace, but he gladly let her cling, feeling the slight incessant trembling which shook her body.

The white shape of the small van was visible some way off, four places from the end of the painted lines of parking spaces in front of the ancient inn.

"Got your keys?" Sam asked Turner.

"What d'you think?" Turner unlocked the driver's door. With the powerful torch which Rodney had brought from the garage they examined the two seats, the glove compartment, and the floor, Sam using a handkerchief to touch everything.

"Well?"

"Same as usual," Turner said. "Just maps and the usual stuff. You'll want the back opening."

He unlocked the double doors at the rear. A powerful, sickening smell of raw meat came out to them. But Jack Turner prided himself on his hygiene, and all the van contained was a pile of flat wooden boxes and another pile of kitchen paper. Sam asked him to bring them out. Under the light of one of the decorative lamps outside the Rose, and examined with the torch, they proved to be scrupulously clean, though the boxes were marked by a few dark stains. Doran stared at them.

"What d'you expect?" Turner asked her. "All been scrubbed, take it from me. Our Arnold only keeps them there for reserves, we use fresh ones for all the meat that goes out."

The floor of the van had also been scrubbed, Arnold's morning routine, his father told them. He stood back, triumphantly watching as Sam crawled in the small diameter, throwing the torchlight into every corner.

He backed out, and rejoined them.

"No sign of anything. All right, Jack, you can put the stuff back now."

Turner picked up the boxes and began to replace them, grumbling at their weight. Doran steadied the corner nearest to her; and gave a cry that made the others jump and halted customers who were leaving the Rose at closing time.

"Look, look." She stood under the lamp with something on her palm. It was a small button, about half an inch in circumference, with a decoration in the middle of it, and broken cotton threads hanging from the back.

"Oh God," said Rodney. There was no need to look closer. He knew that the little decoration was a small bluebird. Christopher's crawler-suit of blue cotton-mixture was appliquéd across the chest with a bluebird in flight, and the buttons, where buttons were needed, bore the same motif.

Doran's face was a mask of horror. Speechless, she held the little object out to them. Rodney, who had never fainted in his life, knew momentarily how an oncoming faint would feel. Sam, who swore seldom, and never blasphemed, said, "Christ," and Jack Turner, peering closely, drew in his breath with a sharp hiss.

Doran said, "So the baby turned into a pig, after all. I always wondered how it was done." On the last words her voice rose sharply into a scream of laughter that shocked the ears, then broke in wild sobbing.

Rodney exclaimed, "Doran!" and clutched at her, but she twisted out of his hold and ran across the road through the glare from the headlights of cars starting up. Somebody said, "Silly cow." A knot of people who had come out of the Rose were gathering, asking questions.

Sam raised his voice, a carrying one.

"Please go home, all of you. There's nothing to see. Mrs. Chelmarsh has just had a shock. We can sort it out better if you leave us by ourselves. Thank you, goodnight." He greeted various customers known to him. Slowly they dispersed, talking and looking back.

Rodney sat down on a low wall, his head in his hands. Jack Turner had dropped his aggressiveness.

"Seems like the baby was there, after all, Sam. Don't ask

me how it got into my van, though, blast me if I know. All locked up, nobody's got keys but me, even Arnold has to use mine. With valuable meat on board and leaving it outside houses, you can't be too careful . . ."

Sam was searching again with the torch, vainly. "Not your fault," he said, straightening up. "Car keys are nothing to villains. I expect they drove it to some point where a car was waiting, so that the number plates couldn't be spotted near Bell House. Well, Jack, thank you, and sorry to have spoiled your evening. Afraid the van'll have to go for forensic tests—I'll start arranging for that now."

"If it's got to. We'll manage. We can use the boot of my car for the moment." He jerked his head in the direction of Doran's flight. "Will she be okay?"

"She'll be okay," Sam said.

Rodney was alone. Sam had gone to telephone, the customers had dispersed, the pub's doors had been locked and bolted and its lights had gone out one by one. A long half hour had passed, but Rodney paced to and fro in the same spot, waiting.

As St. Crispin's bell tolled eleven Doran came back. He saw her, across the road, emerge from the alley that divided the Feathers Inn and its one-time barn, where faint Victorian lettering still proclaimed Good Stabling to be had.

She came up to him where he stood by the lamp, put her hand on his arm and kissed him. Her face was blotched and puffy and still faintly damp, and her voice roughened with crying, but she was, mercifully, calm.

"There you are," she said. "Thank you for waiting. I thought you would. I'm sorry about that exhibition."

"What exhibition?" He stroked the hair back from her brow.

"Well, they used to call it Strong Hysterics. I should have thought hysterics were strong anyway, but never mind. I didn't want to make a bloody fool of myself in front of the Rose's last orders, so I went to church. It was locked, quite rightly, but I sat in the porch. After a few minutes of—going on like I was doing—I settled down. There isn't

96

going to be any more of that, I've decided. Christopher's alive, I know that, and what we've got to do is get him back. Right?"

"Right. You're wonderful. I can't tell you . . ." His voice wavered dangerously.

"I just thought of the right bit of *Alice*," she went on rapidly. "The White Queen and Alice in the wood, and the Queen saying, 'Consider what a great girl you are. Consider what a long way you've come today. Consider what o'clock it is. Consider anything, only don't cry!' And it worked. Good old Lewis Carroll."

Rodney was not able to make any useful comment on Lewis Carroll. Very closely linked, they walked home together.

An estate car was parked outside the gate of Bell House. It was shabby, it was dirty, one number plate still hung slightly askew where someone had run into it. The interior, spacious enough by the removal of a dog-grille to carry furniture, was littered with objects, and looked as though it would smell like an old-time four-ale bar with poorish ventilation.

It could be nobody's car but Howell's.

The man looked down at Christopher, who looked up suspiciously.

He was very tired, tireder than he had ever been in his six months of life, after strange journeying and fitful snatches of sleep, and so much crying, and he was painfully hungry. The face above him was neither his mother's nor his father's. He was too confused to know whether it could be that of any of the kind strangers who had bent over him and talked to him in the past.

It was all too much to bear. He began to cry again, and he had cried so much already.

The man picked something up and weighed it in his hand.

"Oh dear," he said, "I'm afraid we shall have to silence you."

The three of them sat round an electric fire in the drawing room. Sam had driven back to Eastgate, but would be back in the morning with reinforcements. By then he thought they would have had a telephone call.

The warm day had ended in a cool night. Doran felt an inner chill pervading all her body, and from the paleness under Rodney's tan she knew that he felt it, too. She had changed into a warm camel dressing gown, huddled in which she sat curled in an armchair.

Howell poured himself another lager from the third of the bottles he had so far got through, and lit yet another cigarette. He had, by popular request, changed to a milder brand than his old one, the fumes of which had been hard for Doran to live with in the shop.

"I don't see no sense," he observed, "in sittin' up all night, starin' at one another like pot cats, as Mam says. You two get off to bed."

Doran looked at the silent telephone.

"You're joking, of course," she said coldly.

"Not me. If that thing rings I'll take it, why not?"

"You might say something . . ." Doran stopped.

"Stupid? Think a lot of me, don't you. Look, *merch*, I can do a Solomon when I'm that way inclined, and there's a lot hangs on it. You know that."

Curiously enough, she did know it. In the course of making a complicated bargain or dealing with a tricky individual she had seen Howell exhibit an unexpected degree of reserve and tact.

"Low peasant cunning, thassit," he said, reading her thoughts.

Rodney smiled, and he had not smiled for some time.

"He's right, you know. We both need some sleep. We've got a phone extension on the bedside table if . . . if they ring. But you're not going to sit up all night, surely, Howell?"

"Try me. Tell you something, gel, though I wasn't going to. After you came bangin' on the door and hauled me off to the shop I was still knackered, so I locked up and went home, didn't I, 'stead of off to the Port Arms as usual. Next thing I knew it was after four, so I'd had three hours kip. Fresh as a daisy, I am. I can keep an eye on Little Nell now and then, but mostly I'll sit here an' meditate."

Doran uncurled herself and got up to kiss him.

"I'm really grateful to you, Howell—we both are, aren't we, Rodney? It's been the filthiest day of our lives and somehow you've managed to cheer it up. You didn't have to come all this way after Sam let you know, but you came, and we're glad. Thank you."

Rodney murmured, "Thou, who when cares attack bidst them avaunt, and black Care, at the horseman's back, perching, unseatest ... Who said that? Squire, Poe, Calverley? I really can't remember." He yawned lengthily.

"Yes, well," said Howell, "never you mind, and none of them will. I got something for you both to take, and don't say you never, because it's not what you think." He produced from his wallet two pills, each sausage-shaped, each in a cellophane coat. Doran began to speak, but he silenced her.

"I said it's not what you think. Start you off on anything, would I?"

"I believe there's something called crack," said Rodney.

"Yeah, well, this isn't it. Just something extra, that'll knock you out for a few hours, sort of Mickey Finn. When you wake up you'll be okay, no hangover. I got a friend knows about these things."

Doran stood up suddenly. "We believe you. All right. I'll take anything, personally, so long as somebody will answer the phone." She kissed Howell again, and put her hand into Rodney's.

He watched them go, half-smiling. "Dunno why I bother," he said to himself.

Doran was asleep even before Rodney had joined her in bed. She had not even taken off the remains of her make-up, such as they were. He watched her for a moment, then, leaving the bedside lamp on, went to the door of the nursery. It was an effort for him to go in.

There, too, a lamp was on, the little brass candlestick and

99

snuffer which Doran had had converted to electricity, so that Christopher's first association with a comforting night-light should also be with a pleasant shape. Rodney tried not to see the empty cot. Desmond Reed, huge for the folding bed, slept clothed, in an uncomfortable position, snoring gently. Rodney shook his head. Too bad if the enemy had got in through the window, still open at the top.

He contemplated the cherub, no longer hanging drunkenly as the frustrated thief had left it, but propped against the ruined wall. Perhaps it had seen devastation before, in some bombed church, smiling placidly as it smiled now. The combination of the crude, agonized figure on the Cross and the smirking infant struck him more forcibly than ever as thoroughly nasty. Evil streamed from it, and his sense of evil was well developed, after much experience. Touching his own little gold crucifix, he said, *"Libera nos a malo."*

Now that was strange, hearing himself pray to be delivered from evil, in Latin. He had no idea why he should not have said it in English, as he had done so many countless times. Yet it seemed to be right.

He made himself look at the cot now, feeling his throat tighten: the toys, the cheap little rabbit Christopher had favoured more than any, the scuffed voiceless teddy bear which had been Doran's. The antique rattle of coral and silver—why hadn't It taken that?

He was thinking of the kidnapper as monstrous, rather than a human being with the face of Vinadas. He went over to the Carroll display case and took out the figure of the Jabberwock, hearing himself telling someone that he was taking it with him to the radio interview, for luck. Luck! He heard himself telling someone else that the Bandersnatch was even more horrible, a predatory creature with a gigantic beak.

It reappeared in *The Hunting of the Snark*, of course.

But while he was seeking with thimbles and care,
A Bandersnatch swiftly drew nigh,
And grabbed at the Banker, who shrieked in despair,
For he knew it was useless to fly.

100

The unfortunate Banker tried bribes, but the Bandersnatch merely extended its neck and snapped around with its frumious jaws. A clear picture, and not a pretty one. Carroll must have been fascinated and haunted by his own creation.

Bandersnatch. *Kinderschnätzchen.* Baby snatcher.

Downstairs, Rodney listened outside Helena's slightly opened door. Her breathing was audible. He dared not risk disturbing her by going in.

Howell was curled up on the wide sofa. Sleep had overcome him, meditation not even coming a close second. But the telephone was with him, within the circle of his arm. In the kitchen the cat Tybalt slept, but twitched and woke, then jumped out of his basket and went under the dresser as Rodney approached. That was curious. Tybalt had been altered at the appropriate time and had settled down into a state of deep feline calm. Now he was unmistakably nervous. Had he been frightened?

There was no sign of attempted break-in throughout the house. Rodney went back to the bedroom. Doran had not stirred. It seemed to be his night for watching people sleeping.

He put the pill Howell had provided for him into a trinket box on the dressing table, got into bed, and fell into sleep as though over a precipice.

Morning light crept under Doran's eyelids: she was awake. As Howell had promised, there were no hangover symptoms. Her head was quite clear, instantly and shockingly conscious of what had to be faced that day. Someone was ringing the bell.

The caller was Kate, brisk and bright in her nurse's uniform.

"Just thought I'd look in and see Helena was all right. What sort of night did you have?"

"Fine." It was best not to explain why to a medical person. They went to see Helena, who was shrouded in gloom and refused breakfast, even tea. Kate nodded, and produced

101

from her car a bottle of all-purpose liquid food, to be administered in place of regular meals.

"You'll take that when you're given it, or I'll be round with something much nastier. Okay, Doran? Ring me or contact Glen or the doctor if you need anything, anything at all. And best of luck."

Rodney ate a light breakfast with good will, even reading the headlines of the paper over it. Then he pushed aside his plate and teacup.

"Something's got to be decided before . . . anything starts happening. I went the rounds last night, checking the house. I took a hard look at that thing. I don't like it being there, apart from the mess. We'll get it taken away today, without fail. Desmond Reed's going to remove it, lock it up at Eastgate. He's gone up the road for petrol, he won't be long. And Doran."

She knew the substance of what he was going to say, because she had been preparing to say it to him. His eyes were steady, his mouth unsmiling. "I don't need to put this into words, especially to you. This is a shattering business. I won't say that the darkest side of it hasn't come very near to getting me down. But if we let it do that we shall send ourselves barking mad and be no use to anyone. We have to find a way of going on—detaching ourselves—behaving normally, even though things are very far from normal. Yes?"

"Yes. I decided that, too, when I came down and looked at Christopher's things in here, the milk pan, the foods waiting to be liquidized for his breakfast—all that. Courage . . . old-fashioned word, but it applies. I promise not to crack up."

He offered his hand, which she gravely shook.

"A pact. United we stand. He took his vorpal sword in hand, long time the manxome foe he sought. If I seem frivolous you know I'm not."

"I do. In some play or other, World War One soldiers quoted *Alice* to each other in the trenches, to make themselves feel better. I really knew last night that we had to decide on this attitude, like I said after I—ran away. But I

102

might have weakened if I hadn't had that marvellous pill of Howell's. Yours worked as well, did it?"

"Perfectly." He crossed his fingers.

Desmond Reed appeared, saying that he was ready to leave.

"Right. And you've got that object safely?"

"Wrapped up and in the car, sir. I'll see it's safely locked up at HQ."

"Thanks for everything, Desmond."

"Thank *you*, sir."

"I'll see you off," said Doran, accompanying him out through the back door. She thought he was not the sort of young man to investigate the object she had wrapped in place of the cherub. It was a not very valuable carved figure of Abraham sacrificing Isaac, or trying to, which she had kept in the room where she did her own antique repairing, until she could make a minor improvement to it.

Defrauding a policeman, going one better than the Law. Probably a criminal offence. But it was just a chance for action.

Chapter 8

It's part of the Conspiracy

Reed had scarcely left before his replacement arrived. Doran greeted him with pleasure. He had been Detective-Constable Warrash at the time of the notorious Abbotsbourne murder—now he was Detective-Sergeant, but still young, personable, highly intelligent and more than bearable to have about the house.

Warrash had greatly admired Doran in those days. She had struck him as being very much in the style of the sort of heroine who figured in his fantasies, for he was romantic in an old-fashioned way very rare in the modern police force. His girlfriends, so far, had all been fragile-boned, slim and delicate-skinned and pretty, with big appealing eyes. They had without exception proved tougher than he expected, to his disappointment.

He admired Doran even more now that a touch of maturity was added to her wistful beauty. Her figure was a shade fuller but still wand-like, her curls were shorter: they reminded him of the petals of a pale bronze chrysanthemum. And she was in deep trouble, a mother robbed of her baby. David Warrash would make an ideal husband and father some day. The present situation was one in which he felt totally at home.

"I shan't be in your way," he assured her earnestly. "I've just got to fit a recording device to a phone extension, then I shall stay beside it and not bother you."

"Oh, you won't be a bother. We're glad to feel there's somebody here, helping."

"Anything. Anything at all I can do to help." He blushed. It was a habit with which Doran sympathized, being a victim to it herself, and she found it particularly endearing in a young man.

"The downstairs extension's in my stepdaughter's room." She led him along the hall.

Helena was still in bed, slumped down with only her swollen eyes visible over the bedclothes. A rare surge of feeling swept over Doran.

"Come on," she said crisply. "This is Detective-Sergeant Warrash, who's here to look after the telephone end, and he has to do things to your phone. You may remember him from two years ago or whenever it was. Get up, now. Would you excuse us?" she asked Warrash, who left the room hastily.

"I can't get up," Helena muttered. "I'm ill. I've been crying so much I feel sick."

"If you feel sick it's because you wouldn't have any breakfast. I've quite enough on my mind without you, and so has Daddy. You're not ill, just very depressed—aren't we all—but lying about moaning isn't going to improve matters." Doran stripped back the bedclothes. "I'm going to take you to school."

"Oh *no*!"

"Oh yes. Out you get, I'll excuse you a bath this morning."

Within the hour Helena had been deposited in a classroom at Craiglands, its headmistress instructed not to treat her with too much sympathy. Helena was by now sulkily silent, as Doran had too often known her in the bad old days, but at least she wasn't moaning.

Rodney settled himself, though that was not quite the most apt phrase, in the dining room among his books. He would at least try to seem absorbed in them.

Vi arrived for work, summed up the situation, and lent herself at once to the general masque of normality. Howell having left for Eastgate, she announced that she would do out the drawing room, opening the windows with ostentatious slamming-up of casements and flinging out the cushions of the sofa and chairs to air on newspapers in the sunlight.

Richenda called, before driving to the station, to inquire for news.

"Nothing," Doran told her, "yet."

Doran watched Tybalt crouched under the shade of a bush, unmoving, not even tempted out by a thrush feeding its young three feet away from him.

"Oh Tybalt, what did you see? What could you tell us? If you could only speak. 'The one thing I regret, he said, is that it cannot speak.' " What on earth was that, flitting through her mind?

She went in to ask Rodney.

"Sylvie and Bruno," he said. "The Gardener's Song. 'He thought he saw a Rattlesnake, that questioned him in Greek: he looked again, and found it was the Middle of Next Week. The one thing I regret . . .' etc. That what you mean?"

"Yes. How idiotic. Sorry, did I interrupt you?"

"No. I was just going to ring the hospital."

Carole, the hospital said, was still alive but her condition was unchanged. A police watch was being kept on her. Her husband had been there since breakfast but had now left.

"He would," Doran said. "At least the children are going to be looked after, Mrs. Kenney's moved in there, and she's a tower of strength."

The telephone rang. Doran snatched it up.

"Is Rodney there?" inquired the Reverend Edwin Dutton's dry tones. "There's something I don't quite understand about the Minutes of the last PC meeting."

Rodney listened to him impassively, a muscle twitching at the left corner of his mouth. He answered the query composedly. After he had replaced the receiver she said,

"You didn't tell him."

"No."

There was a silence, during which Rodney pretended to study a book by a Victorian footpath-walker. Doran broke it.

"Did I ask you about Jim Fontenoy?"

"Jim Fontenoy. I'm afraid I don't remember. What about him?"

Doran perched on a dining chair.

"Well. I thought he had a very curious manner. Curious in

106

every sense, I mean. He said he'd come to see me—call on me—me, not us. And something very corny about antiques—very, very flowery, in fact I thought he was drunk, and then I realized it was just him. I thought it was a rather odd way he had of being pushy. Or perhaps just shyness."

"I wouldn't call him shy."

"What did you tell him about me, when you lunched with him the first time?"

"I don't know. (And yes, you did ask me about him once before—it just seems a long time ago.) We talked, I suppose, about all sorts of things. You know how I ramble on. I had the Jabberwock figure with me—I remember putting it on the table. That led to discussing gargoyles on church waterspouts, and church decoration in general. It was a very splendid wine, and I wasn't exactly taking notes. Why are you asking me about Jim?"

"Jim, James. What that unfortunate woman said before she died. We've forgotten about her in all this, you know."

"I'm sure the police haven't."

"No, but they don't tell us anything."

"They've hardly had time." Rodney flipped over a page. The telephone rang. Rodney answered after one ring.

"Yes," he answered sharply. "No. I haven't anything to tell you. No. I don't. Please leave us alone." He hung up.

"The local rag," Doran said.

"Yes, snooping. They've got somebody who picks up snippets of police news at that pub they use. Now I suppose they'll pass it on to the nationals."

"Oh no! What can we do to stop it?"

"Nothing."

"Going back to Jim Fontenoy . . ."

Rodney threw down his pencil and slammed his book shut. "Why are you harping on about him? He's a perfectly respectable Station Manager, with a normal background so far as I know. Don't tell me you've got one of your flashes of insight about him, after one introduction, because frankly I'm not interested."

Doran felt a wave of colour rise from neck to brow. Rodney, her kind, loving Rodney, had spoken to her as though she were a stranger, and a stupid, undesirable one at that. She said nothing for a moment, letting the emotion round them settle.

It was Rodney who said, "I'm sorry. That was unfair."

"No, it wasn't. It was just a fancy on my part, nothing to bother you with. Probably just . . . finding that poor creature in her car, after the Dela party. It coloured the whole evening. Parties! I begin to hate them."

"I know. I know."

She burst out, not meaning to say it, "Why don't they ring? Look at the time—we've been waiting hours, and nothing. Are they trying to torture us?"

"If so, they're succeeding very nicely. Making suspense work for them." He was staring at a book, unseeing.

"Can I do anything for you—looking places up, taking notes? It would help. Me, I mean."

He smiled. "Good idea. It might. I thought I'd work alphabetically, from what I've seen already. Like to type it?"

Doran seated herself at the old-fashioned portable they kept for business correspondence. Thanks to an enlightened Sixth Form, she had learned typing and shorthand at the age when they are absorbed into the mind forever.

"Ready? Appledore. Church burnt by invading French six hundred years ago, give or take. Window of shepherd with flock and assorted marshland wildlife. Henry VIII's standard-bearer under the sanctuary floor, in unfastened coffin, according to old guidebook. Very unhygienic, but I expect it doesn't awfully matter now. Brackets, see Romano-British altar at Stone cum Ebony, two miles away, with picture of cows. Correction, oxen. Close brackets.

"Ash-by-Sandwich. Brass of Matilde Clitherow, note, same surname as Scottish martyr, query saint, query The Blessed, was the daughter, that is Matilde was, of Sir John Oldcastle, the first name given to Falstaff, but not, in fact, remotely like him. Oh heavens." Rodney started violently. "Who's that?"

A man was walking across the lawn towards them. He was formally dressed for the heat of the day, and he looked neither to the right nor the left, in a way Doran recognized: the authoritative figure of John Burnelle.

Doran beckoned him to come in through the French window. Greetings were exchanged, perfunctory on the part of Doran and Rodney. Had he brought bad news? His bland smile suggested that he had not.

He accepted a chair, chatted lightly of the difference between the snows of Caxton Manor all those months ago and the present sunny scene, made congratulatory comments about the house and the neighbourhood, touched on Sam's presence at Eastgate and how Abbotsbourne must miss him.

Then he said: "Sam's still on duty. There was a rather messy incident at the harbour early this morning, one dead and one seriously injured—he's in charge of that. But I thought you ought to know personally, rather than by telephone, about our investigations. Nothing here yet, I take it?"

He looked sharply from one to the other. Doran knew that he was really asking whether they had yet had a ransom demand, and if so, whether they had made any rash promises.

"No," she said. "Not a word."

He nodded. "They often use suspense tactics. Nothing to worry about."

Thanks, Doran told him silently. You sit here and don't worry, and we'll drive back to the nick and get on with your nice quiet paperwork. We should be so lucky.

"Investigations," Burnelle repeated. "Working through the night, they came up with several facts. At our end, your friend Mr. Hidley. He was quite reluctant to tell us much."

Doran pictured Arthur Hidley's face, sweaty and terrified. He had been very tightly stretched last time they had met, pleading with her to sell the cherub.

"But it seems," Burnelle continued, "that his contact was the dead woman, Hanna Page, as you knew her, Hanna Moreton according to the electoral register. Aged forty-two, divorced, small flat in Bayswater, actress temporarily unemployed. Last engagement at the Crown and Cushion."

Doran had once, and only once, been in the cramped audience at the Islington pub-theatre, surrounded by uncomfortable people with beer slopping from their awkwardly balanced tankards as they sat, stood or knelt watching with varying attention a modern-dress performance of *Uncle Vanya.* Hanna Moreton must have needed a job.

"Had a boyfriend, as they say." Burnelle looked dubious. "Not quite the expression, but there . . . Younger man, also out of work, profession allegedly interior designer."

Meaning, Doran translated, anything from bit actor with a fiddled Equity card to agency char. So, no marriage that cracked up. Had there been a passionate longing for a child, in whatever had gone on between Hanna and the men in her life, or had that all been acting? Doran was angry at the thought. She had been conned, and Christopher's photographs used as a springboard for crime.

Burnelle went on to say that the boyfriend hadn't seemed to know a lot about Hanna: probably only lived with her on and off, between other associations.

"But we did get out of him that she was seeing somebody else, somebody who both attracted and frightened her. And who paid her well, sometimes. That mean anything to you, Mrs. Chelmarsh?"

"No. But her frock was reasonably upmarket, she wore several rings, nice ones, and somebody had briefed her on antiques, but not well enough. She'd learned some things like a parrot, but she couldn't fill in the gaps. And that car—little Bluebird, as she called it—I knew it wasn't a dealer's car, unless it was a private one and she ran an estate or a van as well. Didn't you learn anything from the number plates?"

"Changed. Numbers unregistered."

" 'This here ought to have been a *red* rose-tree, and we put a white one in by mistake'," Rodney murmured. "Sorry. I seem to keep thinking about *Alice*." A desperate alternative Doran knew, like studying the posters on the doctor's waiting room noticeboard. "So you think Hanna Moreton was just a cat's-paw of Vinadas?"

"Ah. We got on to Mr. Vinadas fairly early in the inquiries. The obvious line was to ask around the museums and galleries, if he was such an extensive collector—"

"—he was bound to have haunted them," Doran finished eagerly. Burnelle threw her a patient look.

"So we inferred. It wasn't possible, unfortunately, to start inquiries too early, since most don't open till ten. But I know they've tried the Victoria and Albert and the Museum of London so far, without success. I'm waiting for . . ."

The telephone rang. Doran and Rodney started towards it simultaneously, but Burnelle, with a long and practised arm, forestalled them.

"Yes," he said into it. "It is. I am. Yes."

He drew a piece of paper and a pen towards him, and began to scribble, holding the telephone receiver under his ear in the approved fashion, and murmuring an affirmation occasionally. Doran saw that Rodney was tearing up a bookmarker into neat strips and laying them in a geometric pattern on the table. At one point Burnelle gave a low whistle of surprise.

"Really? Extraordinary. Well done. Yes, I will. No, don't. Bye."

He hung up.

"The Yard, as you probably guessed. They traced Mr. Paul Vinadas through the University College Department of Egyptology Museum." He consulted his notes. "Gower Street. Obviously he was fairly noticeable at the smaller collections, tried to bribe them to sell him some exhibit at this one—a cano-something, I didn't quite get it."

"Canopic jar," Rodney said. "For holding internal bits of mummies. If it matters."

"Well, whatever it was, they took his address just in case it vanished. He lives in Kensington, Gladstone Square. Big flat, nobody else living there, full of curios, daily help once a week, caretaker's wife goes up now and then to check on him—doesn't think he's too good at looking after himself."

Doran threw a despairing glance at Rodney. If only Sam were here, Sam who would understand what they were going through and would tell them everything, quickly, mercifully!

"And," said Burnelle, shifting into a more comfortable position in his chair, "the curious thing is, Mr. Vinadas is now in hospital. St. Thomas's. Seems he tripped over an

111

uneven pavement slab, fell down a curb into the road, fractured his pelvis. Nasty, but can happen with someone of his age, brittle bones. He'll be in for months, of course."

"When did this happen?" Rodney asked.

Burnelle looked at the scribbled notes. "In fact, two days before that odd burglary of yours. In Great Russell Street, on his way to the British Museum."

Silence fell on the room: a silence in which Doran could hear the clock ticking, a blackbird scolding on the lawn, the distant passing of a car. She was aware of the hands of the clock, which had seemed stationary every time she had glanced at it, but which had now mysteriously moved on. Time was, time is, time will be. Aware too of her own hands, twisting in each other, picking restlessly at a loose thread in her dress, a snag in the wood of the typing table. She thought how hot Burnelle looked, though he behaved so coolly, and how she should have offered to serve him some kind of refreshment.

"So," she said, "that means Vinadas is out of it. I knew he was too much of a cripple to have been our burglar, or killed Hanna Moreton or taken Christopher. Not personally."

"Not personally. And his lifestyle, from inquiries made, doesn't suggest that he would have been behind any such actions. A frailish old gentleman, with very few friends or contacts, who didn't drive, and had a small private income besides his pension. I suppose he could *just* have raised the two thousand pounds he offered you."

"He had an obsession," Rodney said. "The *Vera Crucis. Crux Emissa.* He could have bought what passed for a bit of that almost anywhere in the Middle East."

"Yes, I expect he could." Burnelle clearly had no idea what Rodney meant, but politely dissembled. He took in the degree of their shock and disappointment, profoundly wishing he had not to be present at such moments, or at the one which would certainly come later.

When the telephone shrilled again he automatically reached out for it, a second or so before the realization struck him that the call might be from the kidnappers, who would be put off by a police voice.

But it was for him. He listened, murmured, finally saying, "Well, I'm very sorry. Yes. Get back if he's gone off duty. Right. I'll be back some time."

"Something bad?" Doran asked.

"Not good. When young Reed got back to the nick this morning he was sent to help Sam with the chaps we brought in after the affray at the harbour. One of 'em turned nasty in the cells, stabbed him with a piece of bottle-glass the lads hadn't found."

"Oh no! Is he badly hurt?" Doran asked.

"Rather deep wound—he's being operated on. I'll be questioning somebody about that glass," he added grimly.

To Doran, distressed for the big simple young man who had kept guard the night before, came the thought that Reed might not have discovered the substitution she had packed instead of the cherub, if he had gone straight to the cells. It seemed unlikely that he would be reporting it while being operated on.

And he would not be coming back for it yet.

She was ashamed of herself for the thought, ashamed of her own folly at holding on to the thing with some vague, wild notion that while she had it there was a chance of getting Christopher back quickly—whereas the police always told you not to give in to their demands until they were traced. She would confess to Burnelle at once.

Then he asked if he might have some coffee, and the moment was lost.

The man covered up the small form and turned off the light.

"What a pity we had to do that," he said. "Against my principles. But—the only way. A great reward merits a minor sacrifice."

"Don't be poncy," said the woman. Her tall shadow loomed over his on the wall. "A lot I care, after all the hassle I've had. If I'm not wanted any more I'll blow. Not much time."

Chapter 9

Breath of Bale

The call came when their nerves were near breaking point, and they were not even pretending that everything was normal.

Burnelle had never been in this particular situation before: he hoped he knew how to handle it. He reflected that you had to do some rum jobs during a police career. He was profoundly sorry for the pretty girl who seemed to have aged several years since his arrival that morning, and the man who had helped others to bear agony of mind, and now had to bear it himself.

He disliked having to be sorry, for he was a man who enjoyed the practical and active side of his work, not the emotional byways down which it might lead him. He tried not to look at either of the waiting parents.

To Doran, in a heightened state of sensibility, there was a different sound to the telephone's ring at a little after half past four. She looked a question at Burnelle, who nodded. She picked up the receiver, holding it tight against her cheek, then distancing it so that the others, who had drawn close, could hear.

The voice was male, accentless. It spoke in such measured tones that the age of the speaker was hard to guess.

"Mrs. Chelmarsh. You have something I want. I think you know what?"

"Yes." Burnelle had told her to say as little as possible.

"I expect the police are listening to this, and if so, I can tell them that their interference will only bring trouble. Listen carefully. This is what I want you to do." In the pauses

114

between his words Doran could feel her heart thudding as though it were trying to break out through her breastbone.

"Take the carving to Ramsgate, in protective wrappings. Behind Hamilton Crescent on the seafront there is a small turning called Pugin Street. On the north side of it is a small café-restaurant, La Sirena. Are you following me?"

"Yes."

"You will enter, and place the carving behind a curtain which hangs to the left of the door, for customers' coats. You will take no notice of anyone who may be there. If a woman speaks to you, say that you are leaving a parcel to be collected. You understand?"

"Yes." Doran heard her own voice as an unrecognizable croak. "But Christopher . . ."

"You will then leave and return home. The building will be watched. Only you are to take the carving. *You are known.* Remember this. You will then receive another telephone call with instructions."

A click at the other end. Doran realized that she was shivering.

"Well, I heard most of that," Burnelle said levelly. "Nice clear speaker."

"I heard it all." Rodney had moved close to Doran at the beginning of the call. "What are we going to do?"

"Simple enough." Burnelle seemed completely undisturbed. "We take the thing along, a WPC resembling Mrs. Chelmarsh drops it in, then we retreat and wait. Simple."

Rodney sighed with relief. "Yes, thank God it is simple."

"Simple!" Doran echoed bitterly. "What about Christopher?"

Warrash appeared at the door. "I got that on tape, sir."

"Good." Burnelle smiled. "Thanks to an outsize memory I've got it too. Now what I suggest is, I go back to Eastgate and fix things up, the object being already there. I was going to suggest wrapping a dummy of the same shape and size, but my guess is that you wouldn't object to losing the actual carving, if it came to that, which it won't. Am I right?"

Rodney spoke for them both. "We never want to see the

115

damned thing again. It *is* damned. I've always felt that it was damned. Let them have it, so long as Christopher's safe."

"They didn't mention him. What are they doing?" Doran whispered. "Suppose he ... suppose they ..."

Rodney gripped her hand tightly. "United we stand. We agreed. Consider what a great girl you are," he added rapidly and softly. "Consider anything. Only ..."

She nodded. Her mind was racing: it seemed to her now that she had had an uncanny prescience of all that had just been said, when she sent Reed away with the substitute carving. The same sixth sense told her that the voice had spoken truly—she *was* known, to somebody. They would not mistake a WPC for her. Burnelle, in his complacency, was prepared to do what amounted to horse-trading with a baby's life. She no longer felt that she could trust him to handle this fateful business. Even Rodney was being no help: he was acutely worried, but she was worried out of her mind, and anything she did now would be while of unsound mind, as they put it at inquests.

"Nobody's mentioned this," she said tightly, "and perhaps nobody cares, but Christopher's weaned. I don't make a very efficient cow, it seems, so the clinic recommended a patent milk and an early introduction to liquidized food, and it seems to suit him. How could—They—have any idea of this? What are they feeding him on? He needs very special treatment with food."

Burnelle looked embarrassed. "I expect they'll manage. They did take the feeding bottle out of the warming thing. I don't know what you call it, in the nursery. Some presence of mind, I thought that showed."

"I'm glad you admire them." She was glad to be angry, because it stopped any tendency to break down. "Have you ever handled any kidnap cases before, Superintendent?"

"Well. A few, always babies taken from prams or hospitals by women who were round the twist in some way, lost their own, couldn't have any, something like that. Nearly always a successful outcome."

"Oh, good. Nearly always."

Rodney shot her a look, then said. "Can we hear that tape played back?"

"Certainly. Only we shall need to do it again for an expert opinion at Eastgate."

Warrash brought the recording gear, set it up, and pressed the starting switch. The voice began, slightly more metallic and artificial-sounding than it had seemed the first time.

"Mrs. Chelmarsh. You have something I want. I think you know what?" They listened intently.

At the end Burnelle said, "Not old. If Vinadas were still in the running I'd have said it couldn't be him."

"Keeping any emotion out of it," Rodney said. "It's a thing you can do when you want to state a fact without colouring it."

"Mmm." Burnelle mused. "I thought myself there was just a tinge of some sort of accent, dunno what. But the experts will know."

"Professional Higginses," Rodney said.

Doran felt suddenly that a great ditch had opened between her and the two men. Rodney, Christopher's father, even he seemed not to be suffering or fearing as she was, if he could still make feeble jokes with words. She was quite, quite sure now that she had been right in that mad moment when she kept the cherub back. It was the only high card she held in this dreadful play for her son. She was not going to confess to Burnelle, even to Rodney, that she still had it. What she was going to do, only she must know.

A replacement for Warrash appeared and took over by the telephone extension. Burnelle made encouraging noises, finished a cup of tea which had gone very cold. They saw him drive away and returned to the house.

"Waiting's the hardest part of this." Rodney sat down in front of his pile of books and notes. "Do you want to go on with these? Because I will if you like, but ... would you mind awfully if I went over to St. Crispin's for a bit? Dutton will let me have the keys."

"Of course not. It will do you good, lots." In their present state she knew that they couldn't help each other. There

117

could be comfort in his church for him. "While you're there," she added casually, "I'll slip up to Elvesham and see how Helena's doing at the Firles'." She had thought it better to ask Ruth Firle to collect Helena and keep her at least overnight. Her portable wheelchair was with her at school, and Ruth was wonderfully good at coping with her.

She watched him go. A very great calmness possessed her, once she was alone.

Light rain was falling. She took a coat from the hall cloakroom, stuffing a dark-patterned scarf into the pocket. Then she went to the new guardian of the extension telephone, PC Feather, an older man than Warrash, unsmiling and sparing of words.

"Boring for you," she said. "I thought you might like the papers to look at. I'm just slipping out to see someone and I expect my husband will be back in a few minutes."

The cherub was in the garage, hidden behind a stack of grocers' boxes, with a tarpaulin sheet thrown over them. Doran took it out and looked at it with hate. On a shelf was an old sheet, folded, sometimes used to line the floor of her estate car, Harris, when anything messy was going in it. By its side she put the carrycot, a freshly charged feeding bottle in a warmer, and a complete change of clothes for Christopher, the disintegrating toy rabbit and the dumb teddy.

Rodney's car, at the side of hers, seemed to look at her askance through its side windows, as if implying that she was betraying its master.

"I'm sorry," she told it, "but if I let him know he'll stop me by force. He'll find out soon enough from Burnelle when they realize they haven't got that Thing at the nick after all. I won't go so far as to put you out of commission because that really would be an act of betrayal."

After a moment's hesitation she scribbled on the notepad which was kept in the glove compartment.

"Sorry, I know you won't approve. But somebody has to be here in case they bring him back, and they just might, this way. Love ever. D."

118

She tucked the note behind the windscreen wipers of Rodney's car.

It was after half past five already, and she had two urgent visits to make before the all-important one. Up the Downs to Elvesham and the pretty half-timbered house that was the Firles' home.

"No, I won't come in," she told Ruth. "If you're quite sure Helena's all right."

"Well, not all right, but certainly no worse and probably rather better. She uses you as an audience, you know, Doran, even when her feelings are perfectly real, which they certainly are at the moment." Ruth omitted to mention the suicide threats. "If I think it's necessary I'll call Rodney or Kate Lidell but I don't think it will be. You're not going to be out long, are you?"

"Well, er. If Rodney should ring, tell him I've thought of something else I must do. It might take quite a bit of time. I must rush now—thanks, Ruth, it's marvellous of you to have her and I do hope she won't be too tiresome."

Ruth looked speculatively after her friend.

To Annabella she said, "If I'm not mistaken, Doran's up to something. She goes pink in a certain way when she's getting round the truth."

"The conscious water saw its God, and blushed," remarked Annabella.

"What did you say, darling?"

"Oh, nothing. We're doing the Metaphysicals this term. Poets. I think that's Crashaw."

Ruth shook her head. If she had not known as an irrefutable fact that Annabella was her husband Simon's daughter, she would have strongly suspected her to be Rodney's.

"It's terrible beyond words for those two," she said. "To have a child stolen, not to know where he is—it's enough to make one desperate, and I did think Doran looked slightly wild. Oh dear. If one could *do* something . . ."

Doran drove faster than usual towards Eastgate and into its northern industrial area, through a trading estate and the new houses built for the workers. She prayed that she

119

would not meet a roving police car whose driver would rec-ognize her and stop her. They must know by now.

In the CID office of Eastgate Police Station Burnelle's voice rose about the clatter of keyboards and the voices talking and telephoning.

"I tell you it's not here. Unless Reed took it home with him, and why would he want to do that? In any case he hadn't time after he got here. Where is the bloody thing?"

Reed was not able to tell them. The constable on duty by his bed at the hospital had sat there for hours in vain: Reed, who had had an artery severed by the prisoner's attack, was in a profound dream-state after the operation. Now and then he moaned or whispered, but no words were audible. He was on a saline drip, his bare chest heavily bandaged and his breathing stertorous.

The station was thoroughly searched, and in a cupboard in the property room the carving was discovered. Only it was the wrong carving.

Sam had had a wearying day. He had experienced vio-lence on a scale that had not been common in his manor, and he had never got hardened to it. He had taken part in the long hunt for the missing carving, a certain suspicion growing at the back of his mind, now solidified. He had known Doran a very long time, and he thought he knew what had happened.

To Burnelle he said, "Has anyone telephoned Bell House yet, sir? I wondered if the carving could have got left be-hind . . . by accident."

"What?" Rodney shouted. Burnelle held the telephone away from his ear.

"It's been suggested that the missing object might still be at your house, sir. If you wouldn't mind looking, and giving me a ring back . . ."

Rodney's voice was dangerously low and quiet when his return call came.

"I'm afraid it's not here, Superintendent. Yes, I've looked thoroughly. My wife—isn't here to ask. I'll try to find out

120

where she is, and I think your people should have a look for her, too. I suggest Ramsgate."

Doran was recognized at once by the young receptionist at Radio Dela. Yes, Mr. Fontenoy was still in his office, he'd been in a long meeting which had only just broken up.

"Did he come out of it at all during the afternoon? Sorry, that's a question I shouldn't ask, but I really need to know."

The girl stared at her. Well, really, some funny people came into Dela. It took all sorts.

"Not that I know of," she answered stiffly. "And as it was in the big studio I'd have been pretty sure to see him." She nodded towards the gallery off which the studio opened. "I'll find out whether he's free."

Yes, he was free, it appeared, though just about to go home. Doran was escorted past the studio doors to a blue-painted office door, and told to go in.

He was rushing about his office, slamming things into drawers, piling up papers, doing a hurried tidy-up. She had thought when she first met him that he was like a whirlwind. The whirlwind spun, and paused.

"Miss Fairweather? Stone the crows, what a nice surprise. You look puffed, or something. Sit down. Have a drink. Have anything."

With lightning speed he produced an opened bottle of Beaujolais, and an almost empty whisky bottle.

"No, thanks. I'm driving, I won't. Mr. Fontenoy—"

"Jim. Everyone calls me Jim."

(Not James, then?) "I'm sorry to have burst in like this— it's just rather difficult to explain." His voice was entirely different from the telephone voice: it could never have sounded so measured, so controlled.

"Explain away, explain away." He poured the remains of the whisky into a tumbler which had already been used. "Don't rush yourself, time isn't of the essence, my wife always does salad on meeting days."

(Wife? She hadn't been in the mental picture.) "Well. Will you tell me, please, why you said at that party here

121

that you were going to call on me at home? You asked for an invitation."

"Did I? How pushy of me." He rumpled his already untidy hair. "But I did want to see your various bits and pieces, porcelain and that, and your collection of fans. D'you know, a great-uncle of mine was in what they used to call the China Trade, possibly they do still, though I much doubt it, and brought a lot of pretty things home. My wife's got 'em in drawers, because I won't let her frame them without taking your advice, as the expert. So when Rodney told me he was actually married to you—lucky devil—I thought . . ."

Doran cut in firmly. "Look, I'm terribly sorry. It was just that I've got something on my mind just now, something rather big, and I thought you might be able to help. That you might know something. Just a mad idea I had. I expect you think I'm demented. Rodney will be telephoning you about the—about what's wrong. Sorry, sorry. I've got to rush."

Mad, mad, she told herself as she drove far too fast up the section of motorway that led north-east. Of all the stupid mistakes to make. Jim Fontenoy, a natural Jim and not James, and the mildest of eccentrics now that one came to look at him.

Hanna Moreton's last murmured words had probably been for the man in her life: James, no, I don't want to leave you. Her divorced husband? But there'd never been one, had there. The live-in lover at the small flat in Bayswater? Anybody, but not Jim Fontenoy.

Another motorway exit passed. She ought to have taken it, turned back and gone home to confess to the crazy thing she had done, apologize to Rodney, turn the whole thing over to the police, who ought to be handling it completely anyway.

Except that here was the turn to Ramsgate, Pegwell Bay behind her, the sea an unattractive sludgy grey. The sun had gone sometime in the afternoon, and now a light spray of rain was falling. She set the wipers in motion, thinking guiltily of Rodney and her message.

The outskirts of the town, homegoing workers rushing past her in cars, shops presenting Closed signs. She drew into a curb parking space as somebody else drove out of it, and studied the town map. Left from here towards the harbour, then right, into the small streets behind it. She pinpointed a little square not far from her objective.

By good luck it had two spaces left in it. She parked, removed the cherub, locked the car and peered into it again to make sure that Christopher's belongings were covered. It didn't do to wonder if they would be needed that night . . .

A woman walking, carrying a large flat wrapped object, would be noticeable in quiet streets. The same woman with a coat thrown loosely over her shoulders, and scarf-covered head, as though to protect her from the faster-falling rain, was less noticeable, her burden hidden.

At the end of Pugin Street she stopped and gazed raptly into a shop window filled with electric devices, not seeing any of them. Thank God, La Sirena was there, and open, by its lighted appearance. No sign of watchers: an old man moving towards a pub at the other end of the street, a girl plodding along with her head down.

Doran walked quickly towards La Sirena with the sensation that her back was in somebody's gunsight. It would not do to run.

The window of the café contained an artificial petunia in a shiny pot, a double menu card set out in large purple handwriting, a list of what were described as Beveridges, including tea by the cup and pot, coffee, various soft drinks and wines by the glass. A mass-produced statuette of a mermaid combed its flying hair, peeping coyly into a mirror.

There were few customers, even at the early hour. Three men sat together drinking coffee: they looked as though they had come from a building site and were going home. A woman with a depressed expression had a glass of something in front of her and the remains of a pastry on a plate. She was smoking. A short fat woman behind the counter was doing something to a coffee machine. It all had the look of a French film from the 1940s, and ought to have been in black and white, Doran thought. Not that colour

123

dominated the scene: the tablecloths were of a faded pink plastic stuff, the only pictures were prints of cute but vulgarly-behaved moppets in rags, presumably disporting themselves in the streets of some foreign city.

There was the curtain to the left of the door, as the message had said. Doran swiftly drew it aside and put the cherub behind it, on the floor. A single coat and a nylon overall hung in the alcove. After a moment's hesitation Doran hung her own coat there and pulled the curtain back into place so that nothing behind it showed.

She sat down at a table, on which some used cups and plates remained. Not a compulsive tidier, La Sirena. Nobody appeared to be watching Doran: she pulled the dark-patterned scarf tightly round her head, covering her hair, and with the aid of a hand mirror from her bag applied more lipstick than she generally used.

The woman behind the counter seemed to tire of producing steam from the coffee machine, and turned up a tape of extremely doleful music played on a bazouki. Doran endured it briefly, then approached the counter, smiling hopefully.

"Yais?"

A very thick accent of some kind, hard to guess what. And other thick characteristics, to judge by the dull brown eyes and the blank, bored expression on the fat face, which must once have been pretty. The woman was tiny, hardly five feet, as dumpy as Queen Victoria.

Doran asked for a cup of coffee, and remarked that it was a miserable day.

"I don' hear," was the reply, but it was accompanied by a smile which broadened when Doran pointed to the cassette and mimed deafness.

"You not like?" She turned down the volume.

"Thank you," Doran said. "I just thought it was a bit . . . that's much better. Could I have a cup of coffee, please, black with cream added after?"

"Sure." She turned on the machine, which fizzed out a very hot liquid into a cup which was certainly not made of china. She waved towards a table.

124

"You sit, I bring."

"Thank you." Doran decided to gamble on the woman's boredom and apparent good humour. "Would you like a cup yourself—or something?"

A gleam came into the small eyes, which had once been large and lustrous, at a guess.

"You buy me a *vino tinto*?"

"Yes, of course. Anything you like. And do come and sit with me." She patted the chair beside her invitingly. As the woman turned to select one of a row of bottles, Doran wondered frantically whether she was expected, whether instructions had been given that she was to be treated amiably, whether this stout little person was the chief villain—surely not—or a trusted aide, or a go-between, the one who might speak to her, as the message had said. She had seemed to take no notice of Doran's entrance, or of the cherub being placed behind the curtain, and to have no expectation of anything particular being about to happen.

She approached the table bearing the steaming cup with a plastic mini-packet of cream in its saucer, and an almost-full tumbler of red wine. Plumping herself down beside Doran she raised it to her lips.

"*Salud!*"

"*Salud?* Spanish?" Doran echoed the word, then saw a bright light of hope dawn on her companion's face.

"*Habla español?*"

To the eager question Doran could only say lamely, "*No hablo bien . . . un poco*, er, *solo*," and watch the gleam fade.

"Ah. *No importa.* Nobody speak *español*. Me, I never learn the English good." She shook her head, sighed, and took another swig of wine. It was not going to be easy. Doran tried the approach of flattery.

"You are La Sirena, yourself, er, señora?" she asked slowly and clearly. The Spanish woman threw back her head and laughed heartily.

"*Clara que no!*" From the gabble of English mixed with Spanish that followed Doran gathered something to the effect that La Sirena did not exist, or belonged to the sea (as

125

of course mermaids did) and that she herself was only a *camerera*, a waitress. "Me," she tapped her enormous bosom, "Delfina."

"What a pretty name. A flower?"

"*Si, flor.* My name too Maria-Annunziata." This led on to a flood of barely comprehensible reminiscence about a husband who had been less than satisfactory and had gone away. Doran began to despair of being able to find out anything practical from her. The workmen rose, muttered goodnights, and left. The depressed woman pushed back her chair, stared out into the wet greyness of the street, and went silently out, leaving no tip, Doran noticed.

Delfina talked on. She had apparently forgotten that her new English friend spoke no Spanish. Doran stole a look at her watch. Seven o'clock already: somebody must come soon, to collect the cherub. Did they even know it was there to be collected? And where were the police whom Burnelle would certainly have instructed long ago? What had happened when they found the carving was missing? And what had Rodney done? She was frantically afraid for Christopher, the hostage.

Delfina's glass was empty. Doran tried to think of some Spanish equivalent for "Have another," failed, and instead picked up the glass, smiling and raising her eyebrows. Delfina nodded enthusiastically and went to refill it.

Doran moved her chair so that she was half facing the window. The little street seemed to be empty. Then she saw that it was not. A car was stationary at the end of it, on the opposite side from La Sirena, an unobtrusive car whose outlines merged with the small run-down shop behind it. The whole scene, like the interior of La Sirena, belonged in an old monochrome film faintly tinted, as they were sometimes shown. Rain blurred the café window.

But the car with the two dimly-seen men in it had a last year's registration number.

"It's got to be her," one of the men said. "Trying to blend in."

"Then why doesn't she push off?" asked the other, or

words to that effect. He was tired at the end of a long day, and he had seen it all, stupid women included.

"Chatting up the waitress, isn't she. Hoping they've got the kid in the back somewhere. Like the phone message said, 'If a woman speaks to you tell her you've got a parcel to deliver.'"

The other looked at his watch. Sometimes life seemed to be all about looking at one's watch. "Can't we go in?"

"And lose him, when he collects? Want to go back on the beat, do you?"

The street was quiet and even more boring than the sort in which they were used to keeping vigil. Its stillness was broken by a figure emerging from a door on their side of the street. One nudged the other.

"The collector?"

They watched the tall slender figure, in jeans and sweatshirt, descend two steps and stand looking from side to side.

"Female," said the driver. "One of the opposite sex, as we say. Seen us. Doesn't like us."

The woman was staring hard at them, aware instantly that they were not travellers who had stopped to consult a map or trippers enjoying one of the less-trodden areas of Ramsgate. She looked across the street to the lighted café, to the two heads close together at the table, the scarfed head and the dark one. She said one word, loudly enough for them to hear it through the open car window.

"Narked," observed the driver. "Peeved. Very cross indeed."

"If she goes in we move."

"Right."

Doran turned from speaking to Delfina and saw the baffled person across the street. For a moment, at that distance, they looked into each other's eyes.

Chapter 10

What matters it how far we go?

The person who had come to collect went back into the house and shut the door. Its lock was broken but the catch of the Yale still worked. It was a house under a demolition order, like most of the buildings in the terrace. A few squatters inhabited it: they had given it a miasma of cooking, pot, and squalor.

The telephone in the hall had been vandalized. She ran past it to the back door, which gave on to a weed-smothered patch of garden, and through a gate once used by tradesmen only, in the house's prime. Her long legs carried her to the centre of the town and into a telephone box before the two CID men had got further than the ground floor of the house. As they went through the defaced rooms they knew that she would not be there.

In the telephone box the agent was talking.

"I missed her, that's what I said. She got here earlier than we thought. How do I know why? No, I didn't see it. If you told her to shove it behind the curtain, then that's where it was. Yes, the pigs did see me, and I didn't come out earlier because you told me not to until I was sure she was there. Seems none of it's worked. Not been worth it, has it? What do I do now? You got me into this mess. No, I can't go in there after her, the pigs'll have me, and if that bit of wood's there they'll have it. How did I know it was her in the caff? Didn't, did I, only couldn't have been anyone else, bunnyin' with fat Delf. Okay, it could have been anyone, and this is Operation Louse-up. I'm tellin' you. Okay, I heard. Right. I'm on my way."

Now or never, Doran knew. She put a firm hand on

Delfina's, which had been about to raise the glass again, and spoke urgently.

"Listen, you must tell me something. Who owns this place, La Sirena?"

"I been told not to say."

"Yes, well, I'm telling you that you must say, otherwise you may be in trouble. Who owns it?"

"*Español* gentleman."

"What's his name?"

A mutinous silence.

"I must know," Doran said desperately. "A child's life hangs on it. A *bambino, mio bambino.* Oh hell. I don't know the word." She mimed rocking a baby, then made a murderous stabbing movement at it with a knife from the table. "Tell me his name, and where I can find him."

"*Qué?*" Delfina now looked terrified. Doran pushed a dirty menu card across the table, and scrabbled in her bag for a pen. "Write it. Here."

Eyeing her like a nervous horse, Delfina printed awkwardly MR. JAIME FERRER. "Like film star in . . . I forget," she added. "Old film, man with little legs, lot of dancing girls." Toulouse Lautrec, of course, still cropping up on television.

"Never mind. Does he come here? Is he to come here tonight?"

Delfina shook her head. "No, not tonight. I see him when he engage me at this place. He ask me many questions, smile when he find I am—*ignorante*? I was cleaning woman at a hospital and not like it, so glad of new job. He tell me not to talk to people."

A light was dawning in Doran's mind. "What is he like, your Mr. Ferrer?"

Delfina rolled her eyes appreciatively. "Young. *Hermoso.* Too young for me, or maybe not?" She giggled. "He have little place where he stay not far away, for what he call business purpose."

Of course. A rich young man, a financial backer with business interests in the neighbourhood. A dark face which might have been Jewish but was not. Burnelle's sharp ears had detected a tinge of accent in the telephone message. The initials and the unlikely name. How slow she had been.

"So who is coming here tonight?" she asked Delfina.

"A woman, some kind of . . . runs errans for the Señor. Not nice girl. Very tall, very thin, no *modestia*, not like girls in my country."

"English?"

"I think yes. She call herself Trudi. She not come tonight, now, I think. I see her, over the street." She pointed. "Come out of house, see men in car, policemen I think. She very angry, go back in house."

Doran's mind whirled. Very tall and thin? But the person she had glimpsed across Pugin Street had certainly not been tall thin Penelope, the PR girl at Radio Dela, even in the twilight and the rain.

Delfina turned businesslike. "You pay me, please, for what I tell you. I speak too much, but it not matter, only a parcel." She held out a hand.

Only a parcel. A mere nothing, only a parcel. Doran took a five-pound note out of the inner zipped compartment of her purse. Never travel without money, her mother had said.

"Where does he live, this Mr. Ferrer?" she asked, without letting go of it.

Delfina eyed it covetously. "Very far away—Jersey Island. That all I know."

But it would be enough: a young, handsome millionaire living in a small Channel Island. And she knew him—now. Doran put down the note and two pound coins.

"For the coffee and the wine. Thank you." She had a feeling that Delfina expected more, but to leave more would be unwise. "Goodbye," she added. On her swift way to the door she reached behind the curtain and scooped up the cherub. The last she saw of Delfina was a round open mouth and two round open eyes.

In the street she began to run. As she turned the corner, the detectives emerged from the house opposite La Sirena.

"Another balls-up," said the senior one. "I knew it would

be. One of those jobs, that is. You get after her—I'll go and ask questions."

He summoned local help on his walkie-talkie, telling himself angrily that he should have known they'd never make it on their own, just the two of them with three women on their hands. Women were always complication and trouble. Not that they'd known it would be like that— the agent turning out to be butch, if he could trust his eyes. He wished his colleague luck with the parson's wife.

The woman in the café would be a pushover, he thought. One flash of his warrant card and she would fall to pieces, by the look of her.

But he had reckoned without Delfina's reactions. Fright rendered her utterly incapable of remembering a word of English, while the effect of the wine was to draw from her a torrent of screams, cries, moans, and keening plaints suggestive of one undergoing rape and pillage. A large part of this was genuine, in her blood, a lesser part the knowledge that she had said too much to the kind lady who had asked questions, and that to make up for it she would say nothing at all. When she fell to her knees behind the counter and began an extended prayer to St. Ignatius of Loyola the detective gave up.

"All right, take her in," he told the local men. "Lock this place up. Then spread out and comb the town for the other two." He added some thoughts on the incalculable and slippery nature of women.

Doran was running. The cherub under her arm seemed to have turned into cast iron, and her breath threatened to give out, but she managed to be thankful that she was wearing sandals with composition soles which made no sound. Without the clatter of leather on wet pavements and cobbles there was no reason why any of the drifters in the streets should notice a hurrying woman. It was a nasty evening, not fit for dawdling.

But suppose she couldn't find the way back to the car? Had it been a left turn, then a right, or the other way round? Fool, not to have noticed street names. Frantically

131

she tried to remember from the map in the car what turnings had led to Pugin Street.

Her usually photographic memory failed her. In panic she turned her head, expecting to see a pursuing man, a scouting police car, or like Eugene Aram—the murderer immortalized in Thomas Hood's poem—"a frightful fiend." The memory of that description did nothing to raise her spirits.

Then she saw a landmark, the mock-battlemented building which someone's fancy had made from an honest straightforward Georgian house. And next to it a one-time chapel, now a playschool, children's bright-coloured cutout designs pasted on the leaded window panes. It had reminded her with a pang of the playschool at Abbotsbourne where Christopher was to go when he was three. If he were ever three.

The little square, at last, and Harris waiting for her, conspicuous now that so many other cars had been driven away. She fumbled with the lock, heaved the cherub in with Christopher's belongings, and scrambled into the driving seat.

In the wing mirror her own wet flushed face looked back at her, damp hair escaping from the sodden headscarf. What a sight, and who cared? She had escaped.

She edged Harris out of his space and turned his nose north-west, away from the main streets and the harbour. At another time—any other time—it would have been nice to meander, to contemplate the house where the young Princess Victoria had lived, had two muslin and two plain gingham frocks for summer, had tried on her cousin's fineries and caught typhoid. Did she see the obelisk on the harbour set up to commemorate her "Uncle Kingy" visiting Hanover? What would England be like now if all royal departures for abroad were marked by obelisks?

A telephone box came in sight a hundred yards or so ahead. She stopped the car beside it, and was relieved to find that it still worked.

A police voice answered after the first ring, to be instantly followed by Rodney's.

"Yes. Where are you? What's happening? What are you playing at?"

"I'm not playing at anything. I wish I were," Doran answered sharply. "Have you heard anything from Ramsgate?"

"I've heard that you went to the place and fouled up the whole operation. Burnelle's furious with you for wasting his men's time. Why in God's name did you do it, Doran?"

"I can't explain. I just had to. It seemed . . ."

"Never mind what it seemed, you were totally wrong to do it. Now they've lost the trail, the kidnapper's agent's got away from them. Have you gone mad?"

"I've thought so at times, but on the whole I hope not." She was trying to sound brisk, matter-of-fact. "I rang really, to tell you that I'm on my way to Manston."

"Manston?" Rodney's voice was bleak, unbelieving.

"Manston. RAF and Danair. Small aerodrome. I'm about two miles from it now."

The pips went, signifying that the call-time had expired. She slipped in another coin and went on rapidly, "Christopher's in Jersey. If he isn't, then I really *am* mad and you can call me anything you like. I think I know who the person is who's got him and where he lives, and I'm taking this blasted, accursed carving there. And I know where I went wrong about Radio Dela. I can't explain any more, I just had to tell you where I was, love. Will you bear with me, just until I've tried—"

"No, I won't!" said Rodney violently. "Listen to me. Do you know that . . ."

"Sorry, got to go. I know I'm right." She hung up on him for the first time in her life, got back into the car, and drove at just over the limit. Direction signs were already coming up.

A great expanse of open sky, darkening with evening, acres of flat tilled fields, Richborough power station rising stark and monumental, a granite fortress starred with tiny coloured lights. Fairy lights, the garden party, Annabella . . . Beyond, the dull silver gleam of the sea. The turn into the modest little airport which was more like a collection of

133

farm buildings, a place of tourist resort to view the old Spitfire and Hurricane, and their memorial building, and drive idly around. The once-famous military base wore an air of retired calm, like a dowager too dignified to flaunt her rows of medals for war service.

There were few people about, scattered personnel who glanced incuriously at the coasting car. No sign of planes coming in or taking off, just the odd one lying peacefully dormant. More and more like a farm, cows and sheep browsing or sleeping in the fields.

With growing anxiety Doran followed the signs to a wooden, Scout Hall structure proclaiming itself to be the Kent International Airport Temporary Passenger Terminal, and got out of the car. Few others were parked, only individuals moving about, no scurry of passengers. Inside the passenger terminal a few people were wandering with paper cups, or seated at tables. Colourful posters of the Channel Islands and Yugoslavia were on the walls.

With relief, she spotted a man in uniform. He seemed faintly surprised to see her, more so when she asked him the time of the next flight to Jersey.

"Not tonight, I'm afraid, madam. Shuttle flight on Monday, 1230 hours, is the next. Or there's a Guernsey flight at . . . is anything the matter, madam?"

She was being led to a table in the eating area, gently pushed into a chair, a cup of coffee put before her. She took off her damp scarf and glanced at the unflattering image her handbag mirror gave back. Her face had gone the colour which usually indicated that she was going to be sick. The kindly official obviously thought so too.

"Alas, that's all we can offer. There are flights from Lydd, but I'm afraid even there . . ." An impressionable, chivalrous fellow, he would gladly have flown solo in order to rescue this pretty, forlorn girl with the look of a newly wingless fairy from her predicament. She was at the window, gazing at the small airfield. A few military aircraft, grounded, another, being worked on by four men in overalls, with a British Air Ferries logo. He pointed it out to her as a Viscount 75. A row of helicopters lay side by side, like landed fish.

"Why are those different?" she asked, idly, not really caring.

"Charter craft. People charter the one they particularly fancy. Those two light aircraft are privately-owned."

Doran was watching a tall person striding towards one of the private planes, a very small one, almost a miniature, white, with a logo in purple, *Paloma*. The figure wore jeans and a black sweatshirt, but the walk, the unmistakable female walk, caught Doran's attention. Delfina's words came back to her. "Too tall for a woman and no *modestia*." This person must be almost six feet and moved with a swagger that certainly would not have been described as modest. Could it be—was it possible that Jaime Ferrer's agent was making for his personal plane? He was a very rich man, possibly a millionaire.

Doran shut her eyes tight, prayed, opened them and asked, "Could I go and look at the helicopters, please? I've never seen one at close quarters."

"Well. I suppose, if I went with you it would be all right. Though the public don't usually." She was not the type to be carrying a bomb, she was utterly disarming: what mischief could she do?

The tall woman was now working on the white and purple machine. Her face, at closer quarters, came into the category of not nice, by Doran's standards, a large nose surrounded by features too small for it, hair which had been dark cropped into a short straw-coloured fuzz, gel-stiffened, one gold earring as worn by punk youths, balanced by a nose-stud on the opposite side. Dropping a spanner, she uttered a word never heard in Doran's household, very loudly.

"Good gracious!" Doran said in what sounded to her like very false tones. "I do believe I know that girl. She's not one of your staff, is she?"

"Not ours. I think she's the owner of that—thing." His tone was dismissive. "She certainly pilots it."

"How very fascinating. I must just go and have a word."

He let her go, resigned. You found 'em, you lost 'em.

The expression on the tall girl's face as she saw Doran approaching was not one of welcoming recognition. She straightened up to what was clearly a full six feet.

"Excuse me," said Doran, "but don't I know you?"

"Dunno *you*, do I." The telephone message had said that Doran would be known. A bluff. The voice was deep and rough, not quite Cockney. Gravesham, perhaps, the version of London speech which had come down by water from Thames to Medway. Its owner wiped her hands on her jeans, then with deliberation picked up the spanner and weighed it as though calculating how hard it could hit.

"Oh, sorry." Doran plunged: if she were wrong there would be no harm done. "I thought I saw you earlier, in Pugin Street."

She was not wrong. A look of extreme hostility shot from eyes that were heavily outlined in black, with pink shadow on the lids, and the large fingers tightened on the spanner.

"'Ere, what you want? What's it got to do with you where I've been?"

A long look passed between them. Doran seemed to hear the other's brain ticking over.

"Well, bugger me," said the tall girl. "It *was* you waiting in there, in that caff?"

"Yes. But we seem to have missed each other. You're Trudi, I take it—at least I think that was what Delfina said."

She found herself suddenly looking up into a face lowering down at her with a distinctly threatening expression. Something like an early Walton figurine, badly modelled, roughly painted.

"Where is it, then?" Trudi demanded. "You brought it, or not?"

"Brought what?"

"Don't act innocent with me. Tell, or I'll bash you till you do."

"Oh, I don't think so. That nice young man who brought me out here is watching from the window, and the mechanics working on that plane are very interested." Doran felt

136

her knees shaking and hoped her voice was not. But the bluff was justified. Trudi was a conspicuous figure, and her advance on Doran had not gone unnoticed. The nice young man had, indeed, emerged from the terminal and was calling.

"Anything I can help with?"

Doran smiled brilliantly at him. "No thanks," she called back. "Don't go away, though." To Trudi she said, "You're flying this thing to Jersey, aren't you?"

"No."

"Oh, I think you are. Operation La Sirena went wrong, and you've got to face Señor Ferrer empty-handed. Somehow I don't think he'll be too pleased. Well, I do know where—what you want—is, and I'll get it for you on one condition."

Trudi had stepped back. A mixture of emotions struggled in her, visibly: suspicion, resentment, the dawning hope of a way out of her dilemma.

"What condition?"

"That you take me with you to Jersey."

Trudi threw back her head with a bark of laughter.

"Quite a gas, aren't you. Me take you? I can just see it."

"Well, you better had see it," Doran said reasonably, "because otherwise you won't get your precious carving."

She had lost a point. "And you won't get your precious baby. Remember what *he* told you—bring the pigs in, it means trouble, and you brought 'em in. Can't deny it, can yer."

Doran's voice was trembling now. "Is my baby all right? They haven't done anything to him, have they? Oh, do please tell me! You don't know how . . ." She was out of control, Trudi watching her curiously, with sardonic enjoyment.

"Better come and see for yourself, then," she said. "If you got the wood."

The young official had made up his mind that something undesirable was going on. He appeared at their side.

"Now, ladies, if you're having some trouble, perhaps we can sort it out. Shall we go in and see what can be done?"

137

Gently but firmly, he was steering Doran towards the terminal. She pulled herself together with a tremendous effort.

"You're so kind, but it's all right—this lady's giving me a lift. It's really very urgent, you see—a matter of life and death, you might say. We're just going to get something from my car, then we'll be off—isn't that right, Trudi?"

Trudi's answer might have been assent or a wordless growl. But she followed. On the way to Harris, Doran managed to persuade her worried escort that she was used to flying, that she would be quite warm enough, that she had friends waiting for her whom she had telephoned in the expectation of an evening air ferry, and that she and Trudi had known each other for years. None of it sounded convincing, even to her. But Trudi was a known figure, and had a pilot's licence, which she flashed disdainfully from the back pocket of her jeans. There seemed to be nothing against the arrangement except an atmosphere of danger and menace. Reluctantly he left the women.

Doran unlocked Harris, got out the cherub, exhibited it to Trudi, and before re-locking the passenger door deliberately exposed to Trudi's view the floor of the car, packed with Christopher's belongings.

The girl stared at them, without expression.

"Have you any children?" Doran asked gently.

"Not likely. Three abortions, that's what I've had."

Shuddering, Doran locked the car. She still carried the cherub as they returned to the airfield. Trudi's eyes never left it, as though it might de-materialize at any moment, until, when they reached a telephone box, she muttered. "If you do a runner I'll kill you."

Doran waited, watching Trudi talking to someone unknown. No, not true, someone who had been unknown. Was he as evil as his repulsive deputy?

She was in the passenger seat, watching the reflection of *Paloma's* lights in one of the yellow helicopters lying motionless below. Her fear for Christopher was intensified, sharp and dreadful. She tried to remember a worse moment in her life, and failed.

Trudi was operating the controls with easy calm. Something twinkled on the top joint of the shortest finger of her right hand. It was Doran's own engagement ring, ruby and pearl. So Trudi had been the unsuccessful robber of Bell House, the night the ring had disappeared. She had entered their bedroom, seen Doran and Rodney asleep. She had also been the daylight invader who had taken Christopher and savaged Carole. A mercenary, a hired bravo with no scruples.

Quite possibly she would come down at some lonely spot, kill Doran, and leave with the cherub. Perhaps that was the reason why she had agreed to let Doran accompany her. It began to seem more and more likely.

Doran shut her eyes and thought very intensely of Rodney. Would she ever see him again? Somehow she felt she would, whatever happened. She thought of Howell, more fondly than ever before. He would miss her very much. She hoped he would find a new partner for the shop.

The shop. If only she had never gone to that auction and bought that accursed cherub. It was behind them on a ledge. She could just glimpse a corner of it. How fantastic, trading a wooden baby for a living one. Horse-trading, infant-trading. If one were lucky.

How far were they going? The Channel Islands lay ninety miles or so beyond the southern coast of England, beyond Weymouth. Was this frail-looking, fancy craft suitable for flying so far? She turned to say this to Trudi, then changed her mind at the sight of that snub profile with the downturned lips. What, in any case, was the use . . .

If this were a nightmare, it was the chilliest and longest nightmare ever dreamed. Desperately she searched her mind for something to think of, to distract her from imminent madness. Somehow the uplifting, spiritual subjects failed to work: were, indeed, faintly depressing.

Quite clearly, in her head, she heard Rodney saying, "Carroll".

Of course, my darling—Carroll. Ineffable, divine nonsense. And not any she knew backwards, like *Alice*. No, there was a later book, quite awful in its twee, cute sentimentality, but full of fascinating diversions from the sickly

Sylvie and the repulsive Bruno. Doran had bought a first edition of it, for Christopher's future library, and found it not worth the money except for the songs.

> Little Birds are writing
> Interesting books,
> To be read by cooks:
> Read, I say, not roasted—
> Letterpress, when toasted,
> Loses its good looks.

> Little Birds are playing
> Bagpipes on the shore,
> Where the tourists snore:
> "Thanks!" they cry. "'Tis thrilling!
> Take, oh take this shilling,
> Let us have no more."

> Little Birds are hiding
> Crimes in carpet-bags . . .

But her memory jibbed at what Little Birds did next, though she knew they had a variety of unlikely occupations. What about the person who thought he saw?

> He thought he saw a Buffalo
> Upon the chimney-piece:
> He looked again, and found it was
> His Sister's Husband's Niece.
> "Unless you leave this house," he said,
> "I'll send for the police!"

Curious, how everything, even in Carroll, came back to crimes and police. Curiouser, and curiouser, and curiouser . . .

"You been asleep," said a harsh voice very loudly close to her ear. "Come on, stir. This is it."

Doran shook herself conscious and looked out. The sparkle and dull shine of the sea lay beneath them, and a sprinkle of lights like scattered stars, and, far ahead of them, a brilliant beam of light, slowly revolving.

"The Crow's Nest," Trudi informed her. "You can see it eighteen miles out on a clear night. Bloody good landmark. They've got a bit of sense, the Jerseyaise, I'll say that. We're over the Island now—there's Ronez Point. Kindly fasten your seatbelts, ladies and gents, we're landing."

"But you're not going towards the airfield," Doran pointed out. "Look, the runway lights are over there."

Trudi snorted. "What d'you take me for? Not landin' there, am I. No bloody fear."

Chapter 11

The Manxome Foe

"They can't find her," Rodney said. "So where is she?"

Howell, at the kitchen table with a bottle of light ale, shook his head. He had heard in full the tale of the misadventures at Ramsgate. Burnelle had told Rodney, in a telephone voice which could be heard clearly across the room, what he thought of Doran's rash behaviour, the results of which had now kept him on duty most of the evening. He had mentioned wasting police time, criminal folly, defiance of orders, and the wilful endangering of the hostage's life. He had said that, a thorough search having been made of Ramsgate by the police available, he could spare no more manpower. Personally, he allowed himself to add, he washed his hands of anyone as irresponsible as Mrs. Chelmarsh, who had quite possibly been abducted or murdered, entirely as a result of her own actions. Inquiries would continue, but not, he implied, with his approval. He then slammed down the receiver.

The telephone rang again. A voice from Ramsgate told Rodney that questioning had finally drawn from the woman Delfina Comas the name of Jaime Ferrer as her employer, and that she had mentioned Jersey as his residence.

"So that was why Doran said that Christopher was in Jersey. But why? What's a Channel Island resident doing, kidnapping a child in East Kent, and using a North Kent café as a sort of HQ? I've never heard of this Ferrer."

"Maybe not," Howell said thoughtfully. "But it seems like he's heard of you. You got burgled, Christopher shanghaied and Carole very near knocked off and that actress woman *did* get knocked off. Seems to me Mr. Ferrer takes quite an interest in that polychrome carving of Doran's. Got a bit of the True Cross in it, she said?"

"About as much as there is in this table, I should think."

"Ah. Not my line. So we can discount him being a religious nut, then."

"We've been through all that with old Vinadas . . . Wait a minute. Old V. told us the thing was Spanish. Ferrer's a Spanish name. Is that the connection?"

Howell pushed away the half-emptied bottle. "Tell you another thing. Art Hidley knows something. He worked like a corkscrew on me to get it off Doran and I know he tried her afterwards, but she wouldn't part. Now, I think our Arthur knows somebody who didn't get to that auction in time—someone who's been trying to use him, and when that didn't work took to crime."

Rodney was looking more like himself than he had looked for twenty-four hours. "I believe you've got it. Why didn't we think of any of this yesterday?"

"You were too . . ." he paused, delicately, out of respect to Rodney's vanished dog-collar. ". . . too fazed to tie it all up."

"So what do we do?"

"We follow Doran. If Doran said she was going to Jersey, she's gone to Jersey," Howell stated reasonably. "I know her. You ought to."

Rodney hit his brow. "I do, I do. I should have trusted her. What a sensible chap you are, Howell!"

"I know," Howell replied modestly. "Clever, too. My mam always said I was *athrylith*."

"A what?"

"A genius."

Vi appeared round the kitchen door. "First time I've heard you two laugh this evening. Would you eat a bit of supper if I got some ready?"

They said, to her satisfaction, that they would: she began to slam purposefully about with pans and dishes.

"We can't get to Jersey tonight," Rodney said. "But we can tomorrow if we go from Lydd instead of Manston. I rang all concerned, and there's a ferry that would get us in

143

before lunch. If we go to Manston we shan't get there till mid-afternoon."

"Right. And we call on Arthur on our way."

The Strait of Dover was calm and bright, a few fishing boats plying near the shore, oil tankers imitating stately galleons on the horizon. Rodney's tension was comparatively relaxed since Howell's matter-of-fact presence had moved into Bell House. At least, in daylight, action was possible, wherever it might lead.

Arthur Hidley was in his lean-to kitchen, unshaven, pyjamaed, and at a disadvantage. He was not expecting early visitors. Once he had had a wife—might still have, as far as any non-intimate friend might know. Howell was a non-intimate friend, but he knew that Arthur kept an elderly dog which had continually to be let in and out. The back door needed only a push.

"Good God," said Arthur, grease-caked frying pan in hand. "Howell. And, er, the Rev . . . Rodney."

"Yes, it's us," Howell said cheerfully. "Bit early, I know. Any tea in that pot? Good. We'll have the clean mugs if it's all the same to you. Why don't you keep some of them 1953 Commemoratives that I've seen you selling so expensive?"

"Oh." Arthur was already thoroughly rattled, as Howell intended. His hand shook as he poured tea into chipped mugs which were not commemorative of anything. "I don't like using stock at home. You don't mind, I know, do you, you're so . . ."

"Lavish. That's me. Never mind the profit, let's have the enjoyment. God Bless Her Majesty Queen Elizabeth II. This mug says Scorpio—you Scorpio, Arthur? Very imaginative, Scorpios—I'm a Taurus myself, bullish, you know."

Rodney watched and listened, fascinated. It took one dealer to handle another. Doran was vulnerable in her own trading area, and so was this man.

Howell was adding yet another spoonful of sugar to his mug from the carton standing inelegantly on the table. "If you're so imaginative, Art," he said pensively, "why did

144

you think Mr. Ferrer wanted that cherub polychrome of Doran's so bad? Not very pretty, was it—lots like it."

Arthur Hidley's colour was poor, for so early in the day. "I don't know what you mean. Who's this—Mr. Ferrer?"

"Oh, you do know. And him. There was more than a turn on that bit of wood, wasn't there, Art—there was a big fat profit, and something said about what might happen to you if you didn't get it for him. Not a nice man, Mr. Ferrer. Very impulsive, these foreigners. And with all that cash behind him . . ."

It was a bluff, Rodney knew, but it worked. Arthur set down his own mug, quivering wretchedly. He was a much older man than either of them, and his life had not been healthy. The elderly dog, which had been scavenging on the kitchen floor, sensed his distress and hobbled over to him, laying its grizzled, filmy-eyed muzzle against his shin.

"God, you're hard. All right, he offered me a big cut. Enormous. I don't know why, honest—he seemed to have a kink about the blasted thing. Said he'd heard about it too late to send a bidder to the auction. And he said if I didn't work it for him something nasty might happen, to me or the shop. Well, I had to try, hadn't I?"

"Yeah. Sure."

"But I couldn't get anywhere with Doran. You know that, Rodney. Then he—he seemed to forget about me, and the next thing I was hearing about what had happened to you and Doran, and the baby. I was sorry, really I was. I only wish I could help."

"You could tell us where to find him," Rodney said.

"Jersey, that's all I know. He's a tax exile. Got a place here as well, but I don't know where, honestly. He's not the sort of bloke you ask questions of. But you know that, don't you. He's got interests, people he sends where he doesn't want to go himself and do things for him."

"Such as at our home."

"Well, yes. They could get him for that, only it wouldn't be him, it'd be his cat's-paw. That's the sort of roughing-up I was afraid of, you see—that and fire. How is your girl, by the way, the one he tried to finish off?"

"Still very poorly, as the hospitals say. You don't happen to know ..."

A beady glance from Howell told him to shut up.

"Well, thanks, Art," Howell said pleasantly. "You hear anything else from your friend Mr. Ferrer, you ring Eastgate police, see?"

"Not you?"

"Not us, no, we're going to be somewhere else."

"Jersey."

"If you say so." Howell propelled his friend out into Arthur's small and scruffy garden. "Didn't want you to talk too much. He knows more than he says, we don't want any gipsies' warnings flying about in Mr. Ferrer's direction."

"Gipsies' warnings are usually about a dark man and a fortune," Rodney mused. "I have a strange feeling that Mr. Ferrer is going to turn out to be a dark man, and there's definitely a fortune somewhere."

At Eastgate police station Sam was on duty in his capacity as CID aid. Meticulously he took down their information about Hidley.

"Well, it's a lead," he said. "We'll get on to the Jersey police at once. If you catch the morning air ferry you'll be met by someone. Good luck, lads." He was drawn and heavy-eyed, Doran's old friend and Christopher's godfather, and he only just managed a smile as they left him.

"Doran's car at Manston," Howell said thoughtfully. "No clues in it, I suppose?"

"No, just some baby equipment," replied Rodney shortly.

Howell immediately began to whistle melodiously, breaking off to observe, "Talk about fortunes, I'm losing a mint rushing about like a hare on the mountains, when I could be getting summer Saturday trade." He switched the tune in mid-air, giving Rodney the full benefit of *"Hela'r Schwarnog"*, verse and chorus.

"Just reminded me, what I said to you. *'Hunting the Hare'*, good old song. I got Doran really stroppy once, you know, about that—there was I enjoyin' jugged hare or some such, and she said ... All right, I'll shut up. We're nearly at Lydd anyway."

146

Rodney glanced across from the airfield approach to the cluster of buildings that was Lydd, still dominated by the great church that was known as the Cathedral of Romney Marsh. There were a number of interesting features about it: Cardinal Wolsey had been its Rector when the tower was built, and there was a memorial in the churchyard to a man who had sailed round the world with Captain Cook.

But he had not brought his Radio Dela notebook. He was oblivious to the ecclesiological interest of Lydd. He was oblivious to everything but the thought of Doran and Christopher.

The mini-aircraft called *Paloma* was losing height competently and comfortably. There were great shining expanses of sand ahead, curving round a bay and flanked by isolated towers, some of them appearing to be old fortifications. They landed at a well-lit spot near what looked like a car-racing track, and landed with perfect smoothness.

"Good," said Doran. "You're a very efficient pilot."

"Have to be, wouldn't I. Come on, get out. I'll take the thing now." She removed the cherub from its resting place. Beneath her long arm it appeared no bigger than a dartboard.

At a parking spot near by Trudi unlocked a small car. Doran recognized it as a particularly expensive BMW. She remembered that Jersey was noted for its narrow and winding lanes, unsuited to big cars.

The passenger seat was luxurious, and it was an intense relief to be no longer flying, but she was too taut even to think of relaxing. For a few minutes they drove in silence, inland, through what looked like a pastoral landscape.

"Is it far, wherever we're going?" Doran asked at last.

"Have to wait and see, won't you?"

"Look, Trudi. You've got me here, you've got that wretched carving, you won't be getting into trouble now. Can't you let me off the hook, loosen up and tell me that my son's safe?"

"You mean, he's got all his fingers and toes still, and any

other bits he mightn't want to lose? Or just that he en't been pushed off his perch yet?" She giggled.

Doran was conscious of pain in her hands. She could see them, in the light from the dashboard, twisted together, the knuckles white.

"But you must know. You must."

Trudi leaned back in the driving seat, emitted a long, satisfying belch, and negotiated an awkward corner.

"Suppose I know, I couldn't go shooting me mouth off to you, could I. Got no orders, have I."

Quite suddenly Doran no longer cared what she said. She had reached a point of no return, because nothing mattered any more, if Christopher were dead.

"Bitch," she said. "Great ugly ignorant cruel bitch. You look exactly what you are, which is saying something. You haven't got the qualities of even the lowest sort of woman, or you'd tell me about my baby, out of mere humanity. But then you're so stupid you can't do anything without orders, can you, orders from the boss, or whatever you call him. Anybody else would be ashamed of themselves, but you can't, because you're a psychopath. I suppose you don't know what a psychopath is: well, it's a person incapable of entering into another person's emotions. Psychopaths can do anything to anybody, including murder—as you ought to know—without feeling pity or remorse. I don't approve of abortion, except in extreme medical emergencies, but in your case I think the three you had were probably justified, if they'd have been brought up by you otherwise. And that's something I never thought I'd say." She stopped for breath, and waited for the car to be run off the road and herself flung out and finished off.

Trudi said nothing. She appeared to be thinking, if that was the word. Then she said, pensively for her, "I quite fancy you, you know. Anything doing?"

Doran struggled hard with an impulse to break into wild giggles. But, on reflection, that might sound like mockery. Instead she answered politely, "Not really, thank you. Where are we, by the way? I've never been to Jersey before."

"Never? Thought you lot went everywhere."

"Which lot?"

"Well. All you bloody capitalists."

This time it was impossible to restrain a snort of laughter. "What a fascinatingly inaccurate description. I'm married to a country vicar who's just given up his—job. We live in a house I bought with what my mother left me. I've got an antique shop which is losing money. When I bought this carving, which I wish I'd never seen, my husband had to sell something to pay for it. I've got a daily help because I can't look after the shop and my crippled stepdaughter and my baby, and we had a girl who came in part-time as well, though we couldn't really afford her. Now, thanks to you, we don't have her *or* the baby."

Not given to long speeches, Doran was surprised to hear herself talking so much. She sensed that this particular speech had washed over Trudi, dropping a word or two into her mind.

If only the night had not been so dark. Impossible to see where they were going in this unknown landscape. A good road surface, obviously, long stretches of country, an occasional cottage or church, strange shapes that might be old forts or defence buildings left over from the German occupation.

Then, as Doran noticed that Trudi was driving more slowly, something appeared on the horizon, dark against the night sky. Towers, glimpsed over high walls like the walls of a prison. At closer quarters, they resolved themselves into a random pattern of shapes: some were pointed, gables that could have belonged to the Cotswolds, others battlemented, a few exotic-looking, tiled, almost flat-topped, with little meaningless turrets here and there which could have been examples of English seaside boarding-house architecture: it was a giant box of children's building bricks, gone mad.

The car was climbing towards a break in the high walls. Trudi sounded the horn twice, at which a light came on over what proved, when they reached it, to be a steel door without visible means of opening.

149

Trudi got out and pressed something at the side of it. With an electronic hum the door slowly disappeared, sliding into the deep wall.

"Come on." At Trudi's beckoning Doran got out of the car. Trudi retrieved the cherub, locked the BMW, and propelled Doran through the aperture where the door had been. She noticed a tiny, glassed-in television scanner set into its frame.

They were in massive grounds, lawns, flowerbeds, trees, lit every few yards by lamps, shining high up in the air on invisible standards. Stone steps led up a grass bank to a terrace and the solid walls, rising for several storeys, of the house or castle: impossible to tell which it was. The windows of the ground floor were out of reach. The gleam of criss-cross steel shutters was to be seen behind their glass. Two long windows of the third floor were lighted, as though someone waited up for night visitors.

At an arch-topped door of brass-studded wood Trudi again pressed some bell invisible to Doran. This time the door swung inwards. When they passed through it, it shut with a resounding clang. They were in a stone passage-entrance, modern enough in appearance. Directly opposite was what looked like an elevator, a flat door of bronze-surfaced steel, with four illuminated buttons beside it. Trudi pressed the top one. The door slid back, the grille it revealed followed it, and they stepped into the plain interior.

Not a word had been spoken during their entry into the fortress: or whatever it was.

"A bit Kafkaesque, isn't it?" Doran said.

"You what?" Trudi pressed the top button on the inside controls.

"I said—oh, never mind. Where are we?"

"The Villa Mendoza, that's where we are."

They had reached the top floor. The elevator seemed oddly to have borne them upwards and backwards in time, for they were now in a Victorian landing with wallpaper patterned in large roses. Trudi unlocked a panelled mahogany door and pushed Doran into what might have been an executive-type bedroom in any one of a contemporary

150

chain of hotels. Large divan bed, made up chambermaid-style, furniture to match, open-plan wardrobe cupboards, a door giving a glimpse of a palatial bathroom.

On the bed was laid out, again chambermaid-style, a short nightdress of yellow nylon chiffon. There was no bedside telephone, no television. But there was an electric tea- and coffee-maker and a tray bearing bottles of brandy, whisky, soda and Perrier water, and a terracotta jug which proved to contain milk kept ice-cold. There was even a tin biscuit box decorated with Gainsborough's Blue Boy.

"Well, thassall," said Trudi. "See you." She still had the cherub under her arm.

"But—don't go! Where's Christopher? And Ferrer— aren't I to see him? I've brought his miserable carving for him, haven't I? Don't I deserve some reward?"

"Never you mind about that. You got a nice bed and everything." Trudi nodded, almost benevolently, towards the amenities, and vanished. When the door was shut behind her it showed no sign of either lock or handle. Nothing in this house was designed to be got out of or into except by the will of those in charge. A high turret window was quite out of her reach. Light came from round ceiling apertures.

And there was no point in trying to escape: no point in any kind of resistance. More important to relax one's nerves as far as possible, behave naturally. Her own discomfort wouldn't help Christopher. The bathroom was perfectly appointed with everything from shower caps to Dior toilet water and a white towelling wrap as soft as angora kittens. There were worse ways of being imprisoned. One might be in the Château d'If, in the Fleet, in Holloway. Doran bathed luxuriously, washed her hair, climbed into the brief drift of daffodil chiffon, mixed a large tot of scotch and hot water, and settled down with a pile of bedside literature.

She rejected several glossy if out-of-date magazines and a novel which had just not won the Booker in favour of a thick illustrated volume on the history of Jersey. Just as well to know where one was.

It had all started, apparently, with Mousterian Man. Who? "Fury said to a mouse That he met in the house 'Let

151

us both go to law: I will prosecute you—Come, I'll take no denial, We must have a trial, For really this morning I've nothing to do.'" *Alice* seemed to be inescapable.

Surely that was the same Mouse who told the dripping swimmers from the Pool of Tears the driest thing he knew, which was something very forgettable about Edwin and Morcar, and Stigand, the patriotic Archbishop of Canterbury.

The swimmers would have got drier quicker on the history of Jersey, Doran felt, fascinating as it might be at some other time. What extraordinary names their saints had. St. Helier. Who? St. Sampson, now there's a new one . . . Absently she poured another tot of scotch.

Light still flooded the room—she must have fallen asleep without looking for a switch to turn it off.

But it was daylight, sunlight, streaming from the turret window. A discreet cough, and the clink of spoon against cup, cheerful, old-fashioned morning sounds. A young girl was standing by her bed holding a breakfast tray. The girl was small, dark, pretty and smiling, and the tray contained coffee accessories, toast professionally folded into a napkin, a generous swan-shape of butter and a fine Bow sucrier filled with rough-cut marmalade.

The girl greeted her with a murmured, "*Buenos dias*" and to her thanks for the breakfast tray gave a soft "*De nada.*" Doran decided that it was far too early in the day to struggle with her own minimal Spanish. Instead she smiled, poured a cup of coffee, and realized with a shudder that she was hungover. How much of the scotch had she drunk? But the bottles had been removed, mercifully. The girl, seeing her applying herself to breakfast, faded away in a manner remarkable for such a compact little person. One minute she was beside the door, the next she was gone. Ah, well.

Doran glanced at her digital watch. To her horror, it said 10:40. The events of the night before came flooding back to her—Christopher, the cherub, Trudi, the mysterious fortress where she was still imprisoned. Shocked, she hastily drank coffee, ate some of the toast, showered in a bathroom in which clean towels and soap had been placed, and dressed in yesterday's clothes.

But surely her lingerie had been washed and pressed, and her dress looked strangely fresh? As she brushed her hair with a brush which even in her distraction she noted was hallmarked Birmingham, 1910, from a most elegant fitted case of morocco lined with purple velvet, the maid reappeared, this time quite normally through the door.

She beckoned, and Doran followed her. It was like a sequence from the old Cocteau film. Only the mystical arms springing out from the walls, each bearing a lighted candelabrum, were missing.

The room into which the maid led her was spacious and high-ceilinged. But not, surprisingly, magnificent. As the corridors and staircase had belonged to a castle, this belonged to a manor house. The furniture struck Doran as unusual: she had been to countless sales in big houses, but never to one with a room containing so many chests, coffers, drawers, presses and display tables. The pictures, to which her eyes usually flew, were sparse, varying from the huge to the miniature. Trudi stood by the fireplace, tall, poker-faced, menacing: a sentry.

The man was sitting at a desk, his back to her. All she could see was a bent dark head and a silk gown of Tyrian purple, heavily embroidered with flowers, birds and butterflies, flowing to the wearer's feet, its skirts almost hiding the plain armless chair.

The little maid had stepped politely backwards and vanished again. She must, Doran felt, be a relative of the Cheshire Cat, sharing that creature's talent for disappearing in parts. If one had opened the door and glanced down the corridor, one might very possibly have seen her bright smile, remaining for some time after the rest of her had gone. The real Cheshire Cat had been a ghost, of course, a pet of the housekeeper at an abbey near Carroll's boyhood home, which had returned after death and sat nightly on a post near its old home, smiling in a friendly manner at passers-by. Rodney had told Doran that. Oh, Rodney . . .

153

The man turned slowly round.

"So it *is* you," Doran said.

"Oh, you guessed? How disappointing. I like to astonish people. But then, I knew you were a clever lady."

"Not all that clever. It was only yesterday I realized that you were Mr. Jacob Fraser and Señor Jaime Ferrer."

"Only yesterday. Well, well." The smile of the full lips was as beguiling as it had been at Radio Dela, the olive complexion healthier-looking, on this sunny morning, than in that harsh strip-lighting. She remembered the lazy voice, the merest hint of accent, so soft, yet with hardness in it to match the lurking danger in the lustrous dark eyes, the scythe-sweep of the raven hair across the brow.

"I thought you were Jewish," she said.

"Jewish? Oh, the name Jacob? A version of James. And you were told I had money? No, not at all Jewish." Slowly and mockingly he crossed himself and waved a hand towards where the cherub simpered on an easel. The sight of it inflamed Doran.

"That blasted thing. Why have you put me and my family through Hell, just for that? And where's Christopher? Let me see him this minute. If you've harmed him I'll kill you."

He looked down at the dagger with which he had been slitting envelopes. "Threats don't at all suit you, Doran. (I may call you Doran?) You were meant for love and smiles, and holding pretty things in those very pretty hands. Incidentally, if you were meditating killing me with this particular pretty thing, it would be very suitable. Only the handle is silver, the blade solid steel. It's done memorable work in its time. Do you know, this is the very dagger which made the first of the fifty-six wounds that killed Rizzio, that night, in front of Mary, Queen of Scots? In fact, it was probably the fatal wound. I remember the exact if oddly-phrased words in the history book. 'George Douglas, the bastard, drove his dagger into the back of Rizzio over the Queen's shoulder.' But don't expect to do the same on me—I've taken the rather regrettable precaution of fitting it with a plastic sheath.

"My dear girl, do sit down, you've gone a very nasty ashen colour. Tell me, do you ever faint?"

Doran dropped into a chair, and took several deep breaths. "No, I never do." (Not true: she had blacked out on the day Christopher disappeared.) "I expect that's disappointing for you. I'm not in the least frightened by your version of the murder of Rizzio, who deserved it, I expect. I'm quite strong, though I may not look it, and if I don't see my son within two minutes I really shall go for you. I've been reading up karate recently, and I'm quite good on theory."

Ferrer was smiling. "What a little ferocity you are."

"Not particularly little. I could match you for height."

"In a mantilla you would look charming."

"I don't go in for lace shawls, or even for hats. Where's Christopher?"

Ferrer's smile had faded. "I'm disappointed. I collect new things as well as old: I had thought of collecting you. The women I meet at Radio Dela disgust me, so hard, so masculine. Even those I was foolish enough to establish at my pied-à-terre nearby. I had to get rid of them."

"The way you got rid of poor Hanna Moreton?"

"I'm sorry about that. Nothing to do with me, personally. Hanna was very useful to me, at times. She acted, you know—I mean acted on the stage—I also found her piquant—hungry for admiration, for her lost youth. She had a very unsatisfactory lover, I gathered, a creature who lived off her. She was glad to have my money and an occasional jewel or two—and of course . . . compliments." He smiled reminiscently. "She used to call me James. I very much admire older women."

"Then why? Why did she have to be killed?"

He shrugged. "She was going to warn you. She seemed rebellious, unlike herself—something to do with the photographs of Christopher, I believe. I left Trudi to deal with her—unfortunately, as it turned out. Trudi has a very low level of tolerance."

"Did she happen to mention to Hanna that she'd had several abortions?"

155

"I've no idea. Did you, Trudi?"

Trudi sketched a two-finger salute.

Doran knew that her guess was right. Trudi had jeered at the barren woman who had not been able to conceive even one child, much less reject three. Her own level of tolerance was by now particularly low.

"You cold-blooded cynical bastards," she said, "I hope they give you both life. And that's a sick joke, if ever I made one."

Ferrer sighed, with real regret. "Oh, dear. You Englishwomen. How you do disappoint me."

"Sorry about that. I try to give satisfaction, except when I'm desperate. Speaking of satisfaction, do you mind telling me just why you had to kidnap my son and have two women murdered to get hold of that bloody carving? Why not just approach me direct and ask me to sell it to you?"

He smiled. "Would you have done?"

"Well. No, I suppose not."

"So poor Hanna told me. And if you'd refused, and then the carving had been stolen—successfully"—he glanced coldly at Trudi—"you would have guessed who was behind the theft. I had missed the thing once, and once is enough. Wouldn't you agree?"

Doran had been glancing round surreptitiously. She picked up a bronze bust of manageable size with four sharp corners to the base and suddenly advanced on Ferrer. He was perhaps an inch shorter than herself, in his flat mules of Spanish leather: she was savagely pleased to see a gleam of alarm in his deer's eyes, as he backed towards the desk.

"Christopher, now," she said, "I mean it. I can hit hard—you or her."

He pressed something on the desk, turned his head, and spoke rapidly in Spanish. *"No hay leona más fiera que una linda dama—come de tal se ha de huir."* He spread his hands, shrugging.

"I don't understand Spanish. I hope that was the right command. It better had be."

"I never knew," he said dreamily, "that eyes the colour of crystal could flash. For your information, what I said

156

was, 'There is no lioness more savage than a beautiful woman—from such, one must take refuge.'"

"In that case, what are you waiting for?"

The door opened. The little maid stood there, a tiny Murillo Madonna, with Christopher in her arms.

With an inarticulate cry Doran dropped the bust, flew across the room and snatched him. He was intact, all his fingers and toes present. If anything he appeared slightly better-kept than the child she had last seen at Bell House: it took her a moment to realize that he was wearing new clothes, a deep blue, expensive romper-suit with white shoes and socks, and somewhere there were lace frills. His hair had been washed and tightly curled, and he smelt of luxury talcum powder. He regarded his mother with sleepy affability, merging into a one-toothed smile of recognition and satisfaction. Things in the past day or two had been not unpleasant on the whole, but definitely abnormal. He was glad order was now restored.

When Doran was able to speak she heard herself saying that he seemed to have been well cared for. Ferrer raised his eyebrows.

"He was not properly cared for when he arrived. We had to replace all he had with him, and the feeding was difficult." He said something to the maid, who, with a reproachful look at Doran, replied at length in sad, severe tones, as of a nun reproving sin. Ferrer translated.

"She says that Christopher was not as well looked after as the child of the poorest would be in her village. His clothing was not good enough for a gentleman's son, and he had been imperfectly bathed. When Teresa took charge of him he was in a state of considerable distress such as she had never witnessed before, and she has seven brothers and sisters."

As Doran began to erupt in protest he added, "I must admit that this was due to Trudi's somewhat awkward handling of him—she is not experienced with children."

"So it *was* you," Doran said. "You snatched Christopher and savaged Carole. I thought so when I saw you wearing my ring."

"Yeah," agreed Trudi. "All I'd got was a screwdriver, big one—no good for them fastenings on that wood, but I was glad I'd got it when she came barging in. Bloody kids. Yelled his head off, didn't he, and I'd got to use a ferry flight. I couldn't hold him and pilot *Paloma*."

"We do appreciate that," Ferrer assured her.

"I don't," Doran snapped.

"So," continued Ferrer, "because of some complaints from other passengers, and in the interest of getting Christopher here in reasonable comfort, she, er, gave him a sedative. Unfortunately the results had worn off when she arrived here with him, and we had a lot of difficulty in getting him to take the right food when his bottle was finished. We gave him another dose, much against my wishes. It seems not to have harmed him."

"You!" Doran threw at him. "What do you know about it?"

"I have several children, actually. Not here. So you see I do know a little about it, and I'm not in favour of giving drugs to small babies."

"Daffy's Elixir, I suppose it was," Doran said. "The blessed infants' Daffy, administered by Mrs. Corney to fretful orphans. Laudanum. Opium. Drug them out of their minds and they'll be no trouble."

"That's right." Trudi nodded. "Just what I said."

"*My* child!" Doran held Christopher tighter. "Drugs in his bloodstream, at this age. I'll see you get your comeuppance for this—but you will in any case, with murder on your hands."

"Oh, I wondered whether that nurse-woman died too," Trudi mused with interest. "I thought I might've knocked her off, but I was in such a way, after that thing wouldn't come off the wall, and then the fight she put up—d'you know, she bit me, the cow. Oh, well, there you go. Want your bloody ring back? Here, catch."

Ferrer appeared slightly pained by the explanation, and made a silencing gesture at her. Outside the door something that sounded like an argument was taking place: raised voices, the door shaken.

158

"The gate-alarm," he said sharply to Trudi. "I didn't hear it—has it got switched off?"

She looked, for her, guilty. "I left it to José, just this once. You did say you wanted me here."

"It must never be left to José except in emergencies. Go and see who it is."

Trudi strode to the door and did something to what was obviously a self-locking mechanism. The door opened inwards and four people came into the room. Behind them a tall man was gesticulating and shouting in a mixture of English and Spanish.

Doran flung herself and Christopher into Rodney's arms. Between them they created something of a noise.

Howell said to the police officers behind him, "Give 'em a minute. This lot can't get away."

Chapter 12

... Till what is
Dark be Light

The tall, brown-faced policemen, dressed as casually as holiday visitors, had no intention of letting anyone get away. They advanced with measured pace, while Ferrer's small band of servants edged to gather round him—less for his support than for their own defence. The swarthy man called José who had been shouting outside was firmly propelled in to join them. He seemed to have had an accident to his face.

Rodney had subsided on to a small spindly couch, somehow managing to cram his wife and son into its compass, and holding both in a tight clasp. Christopher, who even at his age sensed atmosphere keenly, thought of crying about the constricting embrace, then decided against it and occupied himself with kicking off his new shoes.

"Detective-Inspector Langlois. Detective-Sergeant Allen," said the senior policeman. Ferrer rose and bent his head graciously.

"Where's Jim Bergerac, then?" Trudi demanded. Langlois gave a token frosty smile and addressed himself to Ferrer.

"Sorry to intrude so unceremoniously, sir. Just investigating."

"I don't recall inviting you to investigate—or inviting you at all—though I think we have met. Over fire precautions, I believe."

"That's right, sir." The fire precautions had been in order, but Langlois and his superiors had been less than satisfied with the extreme security measures taken by Ferrer to keep the public out of his property. From their regulation tour of

160

the house it seemed to contain no furniture or objects of high value, and he was not known to be a person liable to assassination.

"He's financially OK, more than OK," Langlois had said to his companions on the way. "The top chaps know all about his holdings, on the mainland and in Madrid. If a man ever needed a tax haven, he does. They even knew he had a double identity, for business purposes, of course. Didn't worry 'em, purely personal to him. High confidentiality about individuals preserved here, of course."

"But rumours," Allen mused. "Odd stories. That great tall bint—I'm not surprised she's known. Drinks at a pub near the airport. Heard her say a few things, after nine or ten vodkas."

"Odd stories, all right. This is the oddest. We can't overlook it, now we've had orders from the mainland." Especially with one who said he was an ex-clergyman as the principal complainant. Langlois, like so many Jerseyaises, belonged at least nominally to the Free Church, but a parson was a parson. Rodney seemed to him genuine enough. He was not so sure that Howell was on the side of whatever angels were involved, and judging by what they'd heard there was at least one, made of wood.

Christopher, having failed to get one shoe off, started to cry. Teresa came forward with arms outstretched, but Doran warded her off. The girl burst into tears—she had grown to love the baby passionately, even in the short time she had cared for him. Among her sobs she spoke to Ferrer, pulled something from the pocket of her overall and held it out to them, making the sign against the Evil Eye.

It was the figure of the Jabberwock.

They all stared at it, the hideous little dragon with its long scaly legs and fearsome claws, enormous buck teeth, leathery wings, and whiskers suggesting a monstrous prawn. And, to lend a touch of horrid reality, a buttoned waistcoat.

"What's she saying?" asked Langlois impatiently.

Ferrer interpreted. "She says that the baby brought with it an effigy of the Devil, and so she had thought that it must

161

come from evil people and that we were right to keep it safe here."

"But that's only . . ." Rodney began.

"So you did have the child brought here, Mr. Ferrer?" asked Langlois.

Ferrer shrugged. "I can hardly deny it, can I? I will even tell you how, if you want to know."

"I'm not too bothered at the moment, thank you, sir, though I imagine your private plane was involved."

"In fact, yes. Miss . . . Smith here has a pilot's licence. She's done the requisite number of flying hours and is a qualified mechanic. They'll tell you at the airport—"

"Thank you, sir, we know that. We also know that a woman with a baby arrived by air ferry from Lydd. She attracted quite a bit of attention because the baby was crying so much, and her—attitude to it suggested that she was not its mother. The mainland CID think they recognize her description as someone they have on their files." He stared, pointedly, at Trudi.

"Why?" asked Rodney, tense. "What had she done to him?"

Doran put her hand on his. "They had to drug him, I know about it. Let them get on." She carried the still complaining Christopher to the window, where the change of prospect soothed him. The window, she noticed, was not only double glazed but had fine steel bars inconspicuously fixed across it.

Ferrer, who had got to his feet at the arrival of his visitors, now seated himself at his desk, leaned back in his high carved chair, and surveyed them as though, but for his brilliant many-coloured robe, he were their judge, not they his.

Langlois was impatient and showed it.

"Well, sir? This seems to be a clear case of abduction, murder in the case of Mrs. Hanna Moreton and grievous bodily harm in the case of"—he glanced at a note—"Mrs. Carole Flesher. Any comments, before we charge you?"

"Carole Flesher. The nursemaid. You went too far, Trudi.

162

You were told not to use excessive violence. Is she dead, by the way?"

Langlois stared frostily. "Not exactly 'by the way,' sir, but she isn't, and as far as they know at present she'll recover—she lost a lot of blood but she's young. Your—assistant—certainly went too far, but then she's done it before, according to our information. Gravesend—Maidstone—Lewisham—approved school before that. And it's not Smith, is it?"

"You mind your own sodding business," retorted Trudi. "*He* told me he wanted that thing, no matter what, so I went for it, didn't I? Is it my fault? Yeah, I suppose you lot think it is. Wish I'd chucked the kid out." She glared at Doran, who noted coldly that Trudi was trembling, the stud in her nose and her one gold earring shaking visibly, the big muscular hands fumbling as they rolled a cigarette.

Ferrer had not missed the movement of the hands. "I told you never to do that!" he snapped at her. "I won't have that habit in here."

"No? Doesn't matter much now, does it? Go on, shop me, you lousy git."

Doran wondered exactly what their relationship was. Better, probably, not to know.

Ferrer's face suddenly relaxed into the smile that had charmed Doran at the Radio Dela party—how many centuries ago?

"Shall I tell you why I had Christopher Chelmarsh kidnapped?" he asked Langlois.

"If we could get to that, sir." Allen poised his pencil over his notebook. Ferrer rose, the perfect host.

"Would you like me to show you some of my collection? I should be pleased to. Mr. and Mrs. Chelmarsh, and Mr.—? I didn't catch the name."

"Didn't give it. Howell Evans." Howell had not interfered in the scene so far. He had dealt with José outside to the extent of inflicting a black eye, and he was prepared to deal with this slick foreigner or any of his mob, if they got dangerous. José kept a wary eye on him.

Langlois exchanged a glance with Allen, shrugging.

Their police training had taught them about megalomaniac criminals who enjoyed showing off relics of their wicked deeds. He hoped there would be nothing too ghastly, severed bits of corpses, or books backed with human skin, for instance. The young mother was pale enough already, reminding him, in an unusually poetic fantasy, of Jersey's famous pearl industry. He had seen a tiny pearl crown there . . . it would suit her. And her husband looked as though he had already been tortured enough. Perhaps he ought to tell them to keep out of it.

But Doran was already standing with Ferrer in front of a Victorian mahogany display cabinet, Christopher, in her arms, now engaged in trying to eat the Jabberwock. Rodney's arm was round them: he, too, anticipated horrors.

But the cabinet contained, neatly set out and well spaced, a number of what might be called *objets d"art et de vertu.* Howell's eyes went straight to a small boulle bracket clock, topped with a figure of Mercury, a graceful cluster of nymphs and shepherds flirting at its base.

"Dubois of Paris?" he said. "Nice."

"Yes, isn't it. Still going, you note—and accurate. It belonged to Queen Marie Antoinette. Nobody knows why her gaolers let her keep it during her final imprisonment, when she was deprived of even the barest necessities. But they did, it ticked as she was taken away to the tumbril and the guillotine, and it ticks still."

Nobody made any comment. Ferrer drew Doran's attention to a pretty Worcester blue and white teacup, with a handleless cup and saucer to match. "Dr. Johnson owned it. Appropriate, don't you think?"

" 'Swallowing his tea in oceans': Macaulay," said Rodney mechanically.

A calf-bound book, badly frayed, was displayed on a square of buff velvet.

"Oliver Cromwell's," Ferrer told them. "A military manual. His name is on the fly-leaf, and there are texts and scriptural observations scribbled in the margins of the pages. That little book has been through many battles."

"Where did you buy that, sir, may I ask?"

Ferrer turned a bland gaze on Langlois. "At an antiquarian book fair. Shall we move on?"

On a wall beside the cabinet hung a piece of embroidery, deer and hounds running in a forest: the faded silks had once been bright.

"You've positioned that nicely," Doran said. "Well away from direct light. But I think you ought to have a small curtain over it, so that it won't fade any more. They used to do that."

" 'Come, draw the curtain, and let's see your picture,' " Rodney added. She shook her head at him, though kindly. It was reassuring to know that he could still quote, but she wanted to speed up Ferrer's guided tour.

"I presume it's the work of Mary Queen of Scots," she said. "It looks like her style, and that would fit in with the general pattern of your collection, from what we've seen so far."

"Highly perceptive of you. Part of a bed-curtain embroidered at Tutbury Castle. That miniature—quite unknown to any of you, I'm, sure." It showed a gaunt and sullen-looking youth, pale and black-haired, in a high cravat which looked too large for him. "Napoleon—an unknown portrait, but treasured by his mother. It was removed from her body after death."

Langlois had taken Allen aside and was conferring with him. Notes were being hastily written. Doran had her eye on Trudi, who was now sitting in Ferrer's chair at the desk. Her hands were out of sight, and Doran wondered what might be in the desk drawer. Possibly a gun, and there was mechanism under the desk for summoning help. She interrupted Langlois and Allen with the whispered suggestion that someone should watch the girl. Allen hastily moved over, watched by Ferrer. Doran sensed that he had been expecting help from that quarter.

"We do find all this interesting," she said, "and I'm sure that goes for these two officers. But I think it's rather important for my husband and me to know just why you wanted that carving. What was so important about it? I did have a sort of passion for it once, but I can see now that

165

it's less than great, as a work of art. What is there about it?"

Ferrer's expression, like the Mona Lisa's, contained a hint of a smile and more than a hint of calculation. He seemed to be making up his mind whether or not to keep up whatever game he was playing.

"Does it contain a fragment of the True Cross?" Rodney asked. "That is, does it purport to? Because, of course . . ."

"We know there are thousands and they're almost certainly all fakes," Doran interrupted hastily. On an impulse, she took Christopher, now lulled into sleep by their voices, from Rodney and carried him over to Teresa, who all this time had sat tensely crouched, her big eyes going from one to another of them, waiting for doom.

Doran smiled at her. "Look after him for a minute or two," she said. "Er—*guardar, momento.*" Teresa held out her arms.

Ferrer gestured. "Won't you sit down? The sofa—and that's a comfortable chair . . . Don't worry, Mr. Langlois, I have no intention of blowing us all up, and I see that any idea Trudi had in that direction has been frustrated. I merely want to tell you a story."

They sat, Doran and Rodney close together on the sofa, Langlois perched, watchful, ready for a move on Ferrer's part, or on the man José's. But José's battered face was dark with gloom: he had been assured that the *policia* would never invade the Villa Mendoza, and now they were here, and certain episodes in his past would come to light.

The cherub simpered at them. In the brilliant morning light it looked particularly silly. The damaged scroll gave it a shabby air. The Crucifixion seemed even more embarrassingly crude and gaudy, the newish red paint of the blood standing out against the centuries-old original.

But there was something different about it. One detail.

"No," Ferrer said gently. "Not the True Cross. I am a good enough Catholic, Mr. Chelmarsh, whatever impression I may have given at Radio Dela—but like a great many modern Catholics, and particularly those in the Vatican, I

166

am not very credulous about miracles and relics. However, some things do survive."

Langlois fidgeted, still waiting for trouble.

"On the great Shrine of St. Thomas à Becket in Canterbury Cathedral," Ferrer continued, "were many jewels of unmatched magnificence. They had been brought there from all over the world by pilgrims, people in high places, the rich, the less rich, all hoping for a touch of the blessed Thomas's benevolence as a reward. Mr. Chelmarsh will know all about it."

"Actually, yes," Rodney said. "It was said to be a gilded ark, crusted with jewels, so thickly that you could hardly see the gold underneath."

"True. And the most wonderful of all was the Regale of France, the great ruby which pilgrims swore they had seen to glow even after the sun had gone down, in that dark church. How it had come to the Shrine was a curious affair . . . Mr. Chelmarsh, our historian." He waved a magnanimous hand towards Rodney.

"Well," Rodney said, "King Louis VII of France visited the Shrine, only a few years after Becket's martyrdom, when miracles were coming thick and fast. The Prior accompanied the King, of course, and while he was on his knees beside the coffer that held the bones of St. Thomas he noticed an extraordinary ruby on Louis's finger. So he hinted—delicately—that the gift of it to the Shrine wouldn't be out of place. The King was rather fond of it, as it happened, and pretended not to hear. And then, a miracle—the jewel leapt from the royal finger on to the Shrine and clung to it. If you believe that."

"Garbage," said Langlois. "Excuse me."

"Perhaps we do not believe it." Ferrer shrugged. "But the Regale certainly adorned the Shrine from that day—I think the Prior was probably a persistent fellow. And there it stayed until the year 1538, when King Henry VIII was busily dissolving the monasteries and confiscating their treasures."

" 'It was a pity and naughtily done,' " Rodney murmured, " 'to put down the Pope and St. Thomas'. Not my comment, Cranmer's."

"Indeed. Twenty-six cartsful of jewels and gold, I believe, were looted from the Shrine. But the Regale was not in any of them. It went on to King Henry's finger, or rather his thumb, set as a ring."

Howell had been listening with Welsh Nonconformist disapproval. "Could've been a fake, or a spinel."

Ferrer shook his head. "Henry would have noticed if it had been. So would his daughter Queen Mary I, who wore it in a diamond collar. Bloody Mary, as unsympathetic Protestants called her."

"Not without cause," Rodney said. "The fires of Smithfield, hundreds of people burned alive, from blind children to old bishops." He shivered. "She was cursed, like her father and sister and brother. Not a happy family, the Tudors."

"Then," Ferrer continued, "it is not heard of again among the Crown Jewels of England. But it was there, until it joined the Crown Jewels of Spain. It was sent there by King James I, when his son Prince Charles went to Madrid to court a Spanish princess. Jewels, jewels, jewels, all to persuade our Infanta's father to give her to Charles as a bride. But Charles changed his mind and the Regale lay unnoticed, until the Infanta's confessor was struck by its beauty and found out its story. He stole it, and had it built into a church carving . . ."

Doran was staring fixedly at one of the blood-drops from the Cross. The sun had moved round, and was striking crimson fire from it.

Ferrer followed her eyes. "Yes," he said. "I knew it, even before I removed the paint. Such power, such magic. I had to have it, you must see, because it was so much more than anything that was here, all these possessions of the great."

Inadequate, Doran realized. An inadequate personality, for all his money and his Villa Mendoza. A believer in sympathetic magic, a borrower of power from the dead. A failure, as the Bandersnatch operation had been.

168

Marie Antoinette's little clock struck, the silver ghost of a voice, the hour of noon. Langlois rose.

"I'll have to ask you to come with us, Mr. Ferrer."

"I was going to return the Regale to Canterbury. I had that very much in mind."

"Abduction, a murder, grievous bodily harm. Want any help, Allen?"

Trudi was struggling in a grasp stronger than her own, with thin steel bracelets on her wrists, and swearing violently. Teresa, understanding nothing, laid her cheek against Christopher's curls. Ferrer sighed, moving nearer to the easel, and what it held, gazing while he could.

Doran watched the jewel sparkle redly as it had sparkled eight hundred years before in the dark cathedral.

Rodney, behind her, said, "And when Henry raised his big white hand. And when Mary's neck stiffened as she heard of yet another pig-headed Protestant. Force. Psychic energy. Ozzy felt it—I felt it myself. You felt it, only it charmed you—that was the difference. I wonder if St. Thomas's own personality somehow got into it? A complex character, Thomas. And this was both white and black magic."

Suddenly Doran turned to Ferrer, now on his way to the door with Langlois's grip on his arm.

"You were very kind to Christopher," she said. "It was dreadful of you to kidnap him, but thank you for the kindness."

Ferrer swept her a graceful bow. *"De nada,"* he said. "In my country we love children."

"But they torture bulls and horses," she said when he had gone.

"We do some extremely unpleasant things in this country," Rodney said. "Come along, love." He took Christopher from Teresa, who kissed the baby's cheek before parting with him. As she raised her head she saw the little crucifix on its chain round Rodney's neck, and on her sad face a look of reverence dawned. She bobbed a curtsey and murmured something, to which he replied, *"Que un paz descanse, hija."*

169

"What was all that?" Doran asked, as they made their way down the stately staircase. "I didn't know you knew any Spanish."

"She thought I was a priest, and I gave her a blessing. It's about all the Spanish I *do* know."

Rodney's tone was terse: Doran asked him no more. She picked up her engagement ring from the carpet, where Trudi had thrown it. She would wear it again when it had been well washed, and when Rodney had blessed it. Because she knew that the power to bless was still in him: the Spanish girl had felt it.

Over lunch on a terrace in the centre of St. Helier the Chelmarsh family and Howell unwound from the two grim days and nights they had just spent. The sun beat down from a cloudless blue sky, they ate *Crevettes St. Pierre* and drank cold Bergerac from the Dordogne. Somehow it seemed appropriate.

" 'The further off from England the nearer is to France,' as the whiting remarked to the snail," Rodney said. "Why don't we have a few days' holiday? If anybody deserves one, we do." He eyed Christopher, who seemed to have acclimatized himself to variety and was contentedly trying to eat a rubber horse Doran had bought him. (The Jabberwock had been firmly removed.) He lay in a baby-buggy hired from a shop.

"Right. Only I don't want to go to France, I want to stay in Jersey." A guidebook was open beside Doran's plate, with a bright-coloured map. "There's a prehistoric tomb at—there, Rozel Bay, which is outstandingly beautiful, they say. Gorey Castle, really very near here, has some costume figures in tableaux . . . It's amazing how near everything is to everything else, with the island only forty-five miles square."

"It would be."

"Yes. You hire a little car and just drive." She gazed dreamily into the distance, but Rodney knew that the limpid gaze was really directed at their bank account. "Christopher would love Gerald Durrell's Zoo, and the Jersey cows.

170

They have bells round their necks and big brown eyes and look as if they were wearing mascara. And we could try him with a dip in the sea, the sands are silver, it says here, and the rocks are a sort of pink granite."

Rodney made no reply. She regarded him anxiously. Was he taking the bait?

"The Fishermen's Chapel at St. Brelade," she added with a note of desperation. "The medieval frescoes are fabulous. Look, here's a photograph . . ."

"You seem to have acquired a great familiarity with that book in a very short time."

Doran blushed. "Well. In spite of the Villa Mendoza, I've somehow taken to the rest of it. The shops! Tax-free scent, imagine it, and clothes we could actually afford for Christopher."

"Hope they're paying you commission for a line of spiel like that," said Howell with a grin. "He's weakening, keep at him." He drained his glass and pushed his chair back. "I'm going to the markets to see if there's any trade about, and then I'm off."

"Off? Where? You only got here this morning." Doran tried to sound sorry, but it would be such a luxury to be alone with her family.

"I got friends, contacts . . . Can't let business get away, can we. You enjoy your bit of holiday, it wouldn't suit me."

"We can't thank you enough, Howell," Rodney said. "For staying with me, for your moral support, for coming here—everything."

"Think nothing of it, just a day out, so to speak," He ruffled Christopher's hair, which was something Doran disliked people doing, but as it was Howell she pretended not to notice. "See you," he said gruffly. They watched him disappear among the strolling shoppers.

"It's turning out like the Lobster Quadrille," Rodney observed. " 'He thanked the whiting kindly, but he would not join the dance.' "

"Only nobody said, 'Keep back, please! We don't want you with us.' You're not really thinking about lobsters and whiting or anything to do with *Alice*, are you? Or even Jer-

171

sey, though I can tell you've given in to my tourist propaganda. Come on, what is it? I know your face too well for secrets."

"Not secrets, really," said Rodney. "I was wondering how to tell you that I think I've made a stupid mistake in my life. I want to go back to being a parson. Ecclesiology be damned. It wasn't just what the Spanish girl said . . ."

"I know it wasn't. I've known for some time. I think you're right, and I want you to do just that."

She reached across the table and took his hand in both of hers. As their fingers entwined a sunbeam caught her wedding ring and made a golden dazzle of it.

"Good," said Rodney. His eyes said more.

Doran contemplated her ring. "I wonder if the Regale *will* go back to Canterbury?"

"Not if Canterbury has any luck," Rodney said. "I see there's no more wine. Shall I order two Cointreaus, or Benedictines, or anything else that is pleasant to drink, you know—so that we can toast the future?"

A local parish production of a Gilbert and
Sullivan operetta turns deadly and Doran
Fairweather must once again find a killer in

PERISH IN JULY

by

Molly Hardwick.

Coming soon to your local bookstore.

Published by Fawcett Books.

Read on for a taste of murder in July.

Chapter 1

To pick up some silver

Doran and Rodney Chelmarsh walked, hand in hand, through the lych-gate of St. Crispin's Church, Abbotsbourne. A lot of villagers had attended the service, more out of respect for their ex-vicar, Rodney, than affection for the girl whose ashes had just been given burial.

Helena Chelmarsh, Rodney's crippled daughter by his first wife, had been what kindly people called difficult. Her tantrums and bouts of hysteria-induced illness, brought on by her obsessive dependence on her widowed father, had effectively kept him from marrying the girl he loved, Doran Fairweather, the young antique dealer.

Until five years ago. Since their marriage Helena had been sent to day school and had become a reformed character—almost. Christopher, Doran's son, known as Kit, now four years old, had become the focus of Helena's life until a sudden late spring chill had struck her down and killed her within two days.

No more driving her to school and collecting her in her folding invalid chair. No more fear of what it would be like if her progressive disease took her over altogether. No more Helena.

The local mourners stayed well behind, leaving the Chelmarshes to make their way back to Bell House, the pretty Queen Anne house which had been Doran's home before her marriage. It was kinder not to talk to the Reverend—as he still was, since the church authorities had kindly forgiven his resignation from St. Crispin's on the grounds that he could no longer tolerate having to use the new Prayer Book and Bible. Instead he was allowed to act as vicar-in-charge of St. Leonard's at Elvesham, a hamlet up on the Downs, where the congregation was small but active.

Doran saw with pity and intense love the increase of grey in Rodney's brown hair, still thick and crisp at forty-three. Her own delicate prettiness had not gone untouched by the work and worry.

"I wish I'd been nicer to her," she said. "They say one always does. But somehow in Helena's case it was worse. Even when she got more ... easier. I didn't handle it properly. I did love her, you know. Only not enough."

Rodney took off his heavy-rimmed spectacles, wiped them, and gave her his peculiarly sweet smile, which had wrought havoc in the hearts of several impressionable females in his congregation.

"None of us ever loves enough. If we did, we wouldn't be human. But I know how you tried, and what you did. And you gave her Kit—that was the most important thing anyone ever did for her. And now it's over. We have to get on with our lives, and try not to let Kit miss her too much."

Doran took in a deep breath of the damp air, held it, and let it go. The old, old routine exercise for temper or tension or abysmal lowness of spirit. She could well understand why some people got roaring drunk after a funeral, though to a less degree why they found comfort in tea parties with sandwiches and cold ham. But to go home and open the scotch would do no good to anyone, least of all Helena.

"That's right," she said. "It's been about the most awful morning of our lives. I know you've taken thousands of funerals, well, hundreds, but never one like this. Poor you. Poor all of us. but it's over now. So—like you said, we carry on. And you'll go over to Radio Dela tomorrow as arranged."

Rodney looked startled. "Will I?"

"Naturally. You can't go back on the new project. It's extremely important, recording the memories of old people while they're still with us, and using them for a parish history. There won't be many of them left if you don't get on with it."

"True. True. Mr. Beamish."

"That's right. Mr. Beamish. And don't forget to take your recording gear, and your camera. Don't ramble on too much, let him do the talking."

They were approaching their own gate.

"Look." Doran pointed to the neighbouring garden. "The magnolia fowers are falling. Must be the damp spring." The damp spring which had laid Helena under another flowering tree, the late cherry in the churchyard. "Come in quick," she added, "or Perfect Paula will get you."

The Bergs were no longer next-door neighbours, the exotic Cosmo and Richenda, whose designs on Doran and Rodney had been persistent but unsuccessful. What a pity they'd gone, taking with them an element of excitement. There was something stimulating in the thought that if one allowed oneself to be lured into the next-door neighbours' for an innocent gin and tonic, it might end in a fate considerably more agreeable than death, though it never had.

Vi Small, Doran's domestic help, shook the crumbs from a tablecloth at the kitchen door.

"She's at it again, I see," she observed to Doran, who was hand-washing one of Kit's garments. "Sweeping up the petals." There was no need to ask who.

"Wearing green wellies, an apron with a big pocket for trowels and shears and things, proper gardening gloves and not a hair out of place?"

"That's right. Well, she always does, doesn't she, Mrs. French? Not a one for letting people see her in a mess."

"Nor is she," said Doran grimly. "I try, Heaven knows I try, with a rampant child who can be relied on to be where he shouldn't, and a husband coming home at all hours, I really work at it, yet I finish up looking like something nasty from one of those old kitchen sink plays."

Vi surveyed her employer with calm detachment. She admired, with reservations, the efficient Mrs. Paula French though she wouldn't have exchanged Miss Doran for her. (Not Miss Doran any more, of course, though it still said Fairweather Antiques over the Eastgate shop.)

"I shouldn't worry, if I was you. Nobody'd ever think you was turned thirty."

"Thanks."

Vi noted the sharp tone, and tactfully changed the subject. She was herself conscious of the passing of time, but what was half a century after all? Just figures on paper, not the way you looked or felt. She straightened her back, remembering the figures of Roman godesses Miss Doran had compared her to. No need to let domestic work spoil the figure. Every Friday evening her hair received a discreet application of a home shampoo guaranteed to keep it darkly glossy.

"What's Mr. Rodney up to today, then?"

"Oh, he's gone somewhere for Radio Dela — some village in Thanet. Taken Kit with him, thank Heaven."

"That's why the house is so quiet, is it?"

"It is" said Doran fervently "And that's why I'm off to Eastgate as soon as I've finished throwing this recipe together. Black olives? Why do they say black olives? They look like little rubber footballs and I should think they'd spoil the taste of the meat."

"Why don't you let me finish it, and get off nice and early?"

"Oh, Vi, would you? You're a natural-born angel. It's just that I feel rotten about not concentrating on special cooking, but when I follow these recipes they never seem to come out looking like the picture in the book, and I saw Kit making a pile of the last one at the side of his plate. For the poor birds, he said. Strictly for the birds, that's me. Here you are."

She propped up the grease-marked volume and thankfully washed the onion-choppings off her hands.

"Her next door's a cordon bleu cook," Vi said.

"She is. She would be. The only time we went to dinner there it was four-star stuff, all done without the faintest sign of effort in the kitchen and guaranteed to make one feel that she *knew* all we eat here is shop hamburgers and chips."

"But you don't, Miss Doran."

178

"I know, I know. I'm only being bitchy, Vi, some people do that to me and Perfect Peerless Paula's one of 'em."

Vi heard her whistling, slightly off-key, as she ran upstairs. Shaking her head, she gave her attention to the preparation of the dish. By the time she had exercised her skills on it the poor birds were going to be out of luck.

Rodney let the car go its own way across the bridge which was taking him and Kit into the Island of Sheppey. His spirits rose at being in what was almost a tiny foreign country, away from familiar scenes and places. He was on a less than exciting mission: the seeking out of a local antiquary, whom rumour reported to be very deaf and extremely querulous.

"But it makes a change, doesn't it, Kit? From all those old churches we used to go to?"

Kit looked up, gave his father a beaming smile, and returned to his current preoccupation, a little plastic box containing miniature goal-posts and a miniature football, the aim being to get the ball into the goal, though it had been fiendishly designed to go almost anywhere else. In fact, Kit had been rather too young to be taken on many of Rodney's journeys to interesting Kent churches, for the benefit of Radio Dela, and as a cleric Rodney didn't believe in forcing too much church on his son. When they grew up they were all too likely to head quite the other way.

Now Dela was sending him out to discover interesting characters, people old enough to remember the past in their town or village. Rodney had learned to use a tape recorder, which saved a lot of tedious note-taking and even more tedious requests for repetitions.

"Cake," said Kit thoughtfully. "Will there be coffee cake?"

"Now that I don't know. But there's sure to be something nice."

There always was, when Kit appeared. He had his mother's deceptive air of fragility (though he was in fact a robust child), her feathery curls, and large, appealing hazel eyes, and nice polite manners of a slightly old-fashioned

179

kind, instilled into him by Vi, who believed in boys learning at an early age to be little gentlemen. No doubt the village school would change all that.

Kit had survived admirably the death of Helena. His experienced father had gently prepared him for it, throwing out mild hints that she might soon be taken away for a holiday with some very cheerful angels, who were quite used to nursing people back to health and had excellent facilities for it — not quite the seaside, somewhere much nicer. A hunt through Rodney's bookcases had produced a quantity of appealing pictures of cherubim and other heavenly bodies with reassuring smiles. Doran's art books had yielded more.

"Don't let's draw his attention to the ones in the church windows — they're all Victorian, depressing and sexless."

"Which nobody could say about the cherubs."

"No indeed. Why are angels nearly always sort of neuter? Blake's aren't, of course, and the ones in the Wilton Diptych are extrremely feminine and really court ladies, I suppose. But mostly they wear those shift things and halfway hair"

"I haven't the least idea, but I'll think about it. Will they work, that's the point? With Kit."

The painted messengers had worked. So had a series of outings for Kit, valiantly and thoroughly conducted by Annabella Firle, when his half-sister was in her last illness. He had cried a good deal when told that Helena had gone when he and Annabella were out one day, and initially had suffered from withdrawal symptoms: she had done her best to spoil him. Then, a realist like all children, Kit had begun to accept Helena's absence, and gradually was forgetting.

As a baby Kit had been nursemaided by a local girl, Carole Flesher, but an attack she had incurred at Bell House, in the course of an attempted theft, had turned her off the Chelmarshes altogether. When they met in the village Carole looked the other way. She now worked at a supermarket till, a great deal safer in her opinion than being skivvy to a family where nasty things happened in connection with antique objects.

180

That was why Rodney took his son with him to as many Dela destinations as possible — it gave Doran some free time. And Kit was excellent company, being used to the conversation of grown-ups who had never inflicted baby-talk on him. His father had even got him into the habit of reciting works he was certainly too young to understand.

"*Sir Christopher Wren . . .*" Rodney began.

"*Went to dine wiv some men.*" Kit gravely continued.

"*He said 'If anyone calls —' *"

" '*Say I'm signing Saint Paul's' *"

"Splendid now what about Rupert of the Rhine?"

"*Fought Cromwell was a swine,*" remembered Kit obediantly.

"*But he felt quite sure—*"

"*After—after . . .*"

"Go on you can remember it."

"*After Martin Moor!*" Kit finished triumphantly.

"Great. Only it's Marston, not Martin. And don't you forget that one, because your mother and I agree with it wholeheartedly. Ah, this looks like the place."

The shabby little Victorian house was indeed the home of Mr. Beamish, the reputed authority on Sheppy's antiquities. Unfortunately his reputation for deafness and irascibility had not been exaggerated. He affected not to know who Rodney was, expressed deep distrust of the tape recorder, and seemed unwilling to part with any information — if, indeed, he had much, which Rodney began to doubt after ten minutes struggling.

"What about Sir Robert de Shurland?" Rodney asked desperately. "You know, Minster Abbey. The legend of Grey Dolphin."

"We don't have dolphins around these coasts. Ought to know that."

"Well I do. But this was Sir Robert's horse . . ."

"Coffee cake," said Kit, who had been sitting in thoughtful silence, ignored by Beamish.

"All nonsense," snorted the old man. "Just a heraldic convention, could have been a dog or a . . ."

"Coffee cake." Kit's mouth was turning down. "Hungry, Daddy."

"Yes, yes, Kit all right. We'll be going in a minute."

Mr. Beamish's strong spectacles were now focused on Kit, not benevolently.

"What's that child doing here? Who let it in? What's it grizzling for? Get it off my clean chair, I know what these brats are like and I won't have my furniture spoiling."

Kit's polite manners slipped, and he made a gargoylesque face. Rodney shut up his recorder, got to his feet and took Kit's hand, none to gently.

"Yes, well. Thank you, Mr. Beamish, we won't trouble you anymore. I'm sure you're tired."

Recriminations were pointless. Kit knew his father well enough to sense displeasure. Rodney drove on to the next village, where a shop provided filled rolls and mass-produced individual apple pies. Informing Kit that they would be eaten later, he carried on across the Island, to its north-western tip, Warden Point. There he stopped and they picnicked on the cliffs, surrounded by hopeful screaming gulls.

The sea was a shimmering expanse, tha dark green of marble, great planes of stormy grey and streaks of silver, as though shoals of fish were emigrating into the North Sea. Not a gleam of blue, for there was none in the skies. Just another English summer.

"You can get out and run about," he told Kit, "so long as you don't go near the road or the edge of the cliff. I'll be watching, mind."

Kit ran off joyfully, scattering crust from his roll to lure the hovering gulls. Rodney sat on in the car, under the colourless sky, thinking colourless thoughts.

The interview with Beamish had gone wrong. It seemed he was unable to deal with a difficult old man on behalf of a second-rate radio station — he who had so many years' experience of difficult people and complex organizations, not the least of them his own Church.

But his church had rejected him — had let him go, then taken him back on sufferance, in charge of a very small

182

parish which one day it would decide to abandon. He saw an enormous fabric repair bill looming, for St. Leonard's crumbling tower and the broken guttering which was sending down rainwater to erode the north wall. The authorities would do nothing about that, and he could do nothing about it himself.

He couldn't afford a nanny for Kit, to set Doran free full time for her own profession, which he knew she missed. But for her partner Howell Evans's businesslike running of the shop, there would be very little income from it. That could be doubled if Doran were freed.

He had been glad to see Helena's battery-operated wheelchair go when she had no more use for it. *Glad.* A daughter lost and a bit of money gained. Sitting in the car with both doors open in case Kit should need rescuing from anything, he felt all of his forty-three years and more. He thought of his father, who had expected so much from his clever only son. He thought of Doran, who also must have expected a different kind of marriage, and here she was married to a failure, a girl who might have attracted someone brilliant in her own line, someone who could have given her a setting worthy of her, comfort, money . . .

But Doran wasn't a girl any more.

Kit ran up to him, holding something carefully in both hands.

"Daddy, look. A snail!"

The snail was a dead crab in an extremely poor state of preservation. Rodney examined it from as far away as possible. "You know darling, I don't believe it's very well. I think it needs rest. Put it down over there and arrange some stones over it. Then come back and I'll wipe your hands with a tissue."

"Poor snail." Kit carried it tenderly away. As he buried it, he crooned a small tuneless song, one of his own making which he often sang. Doran thought he was going to be musical. Well, that would be something for Dad's old age. My son the well-known . . . tenor? cellist? conductor? pop singer? No, that would hardly involve music.

Depressed by this thought, Rodney gazed at the cliff

edge and tried to cheer himself with the thought that the cliffs were packed with fossils. Then he dredged up from his store of useless knowledge the fact that somebody had once built a church at Warden Point, out of the stones of old London Bridge, of all things.

It was not there now. Later Victorians had demolished it to stop it sliding over the crumbling cliff, but the graves of its little churchyard slowly and gruesomely descended to the beach. Even later, tourists picked up bones and took them home as souvenirs. Rodney shuddered.

It began to rain. Yes, this was the English summer all right.

"Come on, Kit," he called. "Time to go home."

In the car Kit was quiet, as though his father's melancholy had passed itself on to him. After a few minutes he said reflectively, "Nasty man didn't have coffee cake. Bad."

"He wasn't nasty, darling. Only old and tired. Never mind, I shan't get like that just yet. I hope."

Kit pondered, then laughed. "Funny Daddy."

"That's right, son. The jester with a breaking heart, that's your papa. Good Heavens, what rubbish. Take no notice. Here, have another go at this." He handed over the mini-football game. "You just might score."

A local parish production of
a Gilbert and Sullivan operetta turns deadly
and Doran Fairweather must once again
find a killer in

PERISH
IN
JULY

by

Mollie Hardwick.

Coming soon to your local bookstore.
Published by Fawcett Books.

Read on for a taste of murder in July.

Also by

MOLLIE HARDWICK

Available in bookstores everywhere.
Published by Fawcett Books.